D0015595

Forever Neverland

———— ★ ✸ ★ ————

Another Magical Book from Susan Adrian

———— ★ ✸ ★ ————

Nutcracked

Forever Neverland

Susan Adrian

✦ ✦ ✦

RANDOM HOUSE 🏠 New York

Text copyright © 2019 by Susan Adrian
Jacket art copyright © 2019 by George Ermos

All rights reserved. Published in the United States by Random House Children's Books, a division of Penguin Random House LLC, New York.

Random House and the colophon are registered trademarks of Penguin Random House LLC.

Visit us on the Web! rhcbooks.com

Educators and librarians, for a variety of teaching tools, visit us at RHTeachersLibrarians.com

Library of Congress Cataloging-in-Publication Data
Name: Adrian, Susan, author.
Title: Forever Neverland / Susan Adrian.
Description: First edition. | New York: Random House, [2019] | Summary: Told in two voices, Clover, twelve, and her autistic brother Fergus, eleven, discover they are descended from Wendy Darling and set off with Peter Pan for adventures in Neverland.
Identifiers: LCCN 2018025631 | ISBN 978-0-525-57926-7 (trade) | ISBN 978-0-525-57927-4 (lib. bdg.) | ISBN 978-0-525-57928-1 (ebook)
Subjects: | CYAC: Adventure and adventurers—Fiction. | Brothers and sisters—Fiction. | Autism—Fiction. | Characters in literature—Fiction. | Mythology, Greek—Fiction.
Classification: LCC PZ7.A273 For 2019 | DDC [Fic]—dc23

Printed in the United States of America
10 9 8 7 6 5 4 3 2 1
First Edition

Random House Children's Books
supports the First Amendment and celebrates the right to read.

For all the kids who may seem
"different" from the outside:
You are perfect as you are.

———————— ★ ✹ ★ ————————

Cast of Characters

CLOVER, 12, loves to sing and secretly wishes to join a choir; a little anxious and bossy, especially to her brother

FERGUS, 11, passionate about mythology, particularly Greek and Roman; thoughtful and observant

GREAT-AUNT TILLY, an old family friend

GRANDMOTHER, Margaret, granddaughter of Wendy; had great adventures in Neverland as a child

GRANDFATHER, Jack, a nonbeliever in Neverland and a bit prickly

MOM, Gwen, close to achieving her dream of becoming a lawyer

THE PIXIES

NARI, DONAR, and GLA, pixies who live in Neverland but travel with Peter to London (pixies are neither male nor female)

THE LOST BOYS

FRIENDLY, gentle and kind, as his name suggests; the oldest in the group

SHOE, one of the only ones with memories of her mother; loves adventure and is good at fixing things

JUMPER, always up for mischief (jumping into trouble); wears her hair in two curly tails

GEORGE, serious and quiet; recently abducted by pirate ghosts

RELLA, little but fierce; questions everything

SWIM, small and scraggly, with long blond hair; the youngest of the Lost Boys

The Mermaids

SERENA, the leader of the mermaids; friends with Peter

JASMINA, competitive about her singing

ALLORA, sweet and helpful

From Greek Mythology

SCYLLA, a Greek woman who was turned into a sea monster thousands of years ago

CIRCE, a powerful sea witch

and, of course . . .

PETER PAN

SKULL ISLAND

TOP HAT ISLAND

N

W E

S

NEVERLAND

1

Clover

I recognize Grandmother and Grandfather from the pictures Mom has on her nightstand, even before Great-Aunt Tilly points them out. They're standing by a sign that says NORTH MEETING POINT, looking the other way. The airport bustle flows around them like a river around two serene boulders.

My heart tries to fly out of my chest. I stop walking without even meaning to, and Fergus stops with me. Great-Aunt Tilly doesn't notice, rushing forward to give Grandmother a hug.

"It's okay," I say to Fergus. "It's going to be okay. We'll get along fine. It's only three weeks."

It's an echo of what Great-Aunt Tilly has been telling us the whole flight, what Mom told us since they planned all this: a three-week trip to London to visit grandparents we've never met, so Mom can take the bar exam and finally become a lawyer. She's been working for this for a long time, and she just needs a final push. That's what she said. One final push by herself to study and take the test, and a great chance for us to get to know our grandparents. They offered. They paid. It's high time, Mom said.

What if they hate us?

Humming over all the noise, Fergus stares at the gray-and-pink carpet. "It'll be okay," I whisper. I stare hard at Grandmother and Grandfather, trying to see what they're like.

Grandfather is impressively tall and skinny, and stern-looking. He reminds me of a magician, like he should be swirling a cloak around his shoulders. He has a burst of wild white hair and a long nose, with strong lines around his mouth. Suddenly he returns my look, and I flinch. He has the kind of sharp, steel gaze that makes me want to lift my chin and stand taller. Or run away.

We can't run away. Not now. It's too late for that.

Grandmother is swallowed up in Great-Aunt Tilly's hug, but I can see her face. She's smaller, softer, and she looks like Mom. Same eyes, that bright blue that neither of us kids got. Her hair is twisted into a low black-and-gray bun.

They're dressed way fancier than most people in San Diego. Grandmother is wearing a long cream-colored skirt with a shiny green shirt and holds a matching green purse. Grandfather has on dressy pants and a button-down shirt.

It makes me feel awkward in the Walmart leggings I just got, and I realize again how ratty Fergus's gray Tardis T-shirt is. It's his favorite, even though it's baggy and has holes in it, and there was no way he was wearing anything else.

Great-Aunt Tilly smiles and gestures us over, so I smile nervously and step forward.

"Hello. It's nice to see you," I say, a little stiffly. I planned it on the plane. *Nice to meet you* might sound like I'm mad we never met them before. Anything else would sound fake. I want to start on the right note.

Grandmother wraps me up in a hug. She smells like perfume, sweet and flowery. It's nice, and I relax into it. Fergus comes over too, but he still keeps his gaze focused on the carpet as he taps his fingers against his leg. He doesn't say anything.

"Good to see you children," Grandfather booms in

his English accent. "Better late than never, eh?" He ruffles Fergus's hair.

Fergus squints and steps back. "Don't touch my head, please," he says, low. Grandfather takes a breath, looks at me, and nods. That's all. No hug or any welcome. Just a nod. I bristle a little.

Fergus is eleven months younger than me—we're practically twins—and autistic. A lot of people don't get that, get *him*. He thinks differently from neurotypical people, and acts differently sometimes. But he's really just Fergus. I wish other people would understand that. I wish they wouldn't stare, or make comments, or treat him like he's not smart. He's just as smart as everyone else. Probably smarter, in most cases. Only different.

I promised Mom I'd protect him while we're here. He doesn't have to have his hair ruffled if he doesn't want to. I frown at Grandfather.

Grandmother tucks her arm in mine and pats my hand. "We are so very thrilled to have you, Clover. *Both* of you." She smiles at Fergus, and her cheeks wrinkle softly. Her voice is warm, her accent making all the words round. "This is a very special treat for us, long overdue. We are going to have a *lovely* time together. Now let's get you both home. You must be hungry, and so tired."

My stomach growls as if it's replying to her, and she laughs. "We'll get on, then. Tilly, will you come with us for a cup of tea before the trip home?"

Great-Aunt Tilly shakes her head, her white curls bouncing. "My train is in an hour. I'd dearly love to get home and see the cats. I'll leave you to get to know each other." She pats my shoulder—and suddenly I don't want her to leave at all. She's the only person we know in this whole country. She's visited us in San Diego lots of times. She knows us.

The panic must show in my face, because she leans over and kisses my forehead. "I'll visit when your mum comes to pick you up. Enjoy your trip. You'll never have a better time. Trust me." She and Grandmother smile at each other.

"Thank you for everything," I say.

Great-Aunt Tilly grins. "You did well, both of you, coming all the way here." She hesitates, then nods once. "Happy thoughts." She picks up her bag and heads off. Just like that, she's gone, vanished in the crowd.

"Let's go home," Grandmother says, tugging on my arm.

I turn back to check on Fergus. "Fergus? Are you ready?"

He doesn't answer, his eyes still fixed on the floor.

He's breathing a little fast. It's been a long, long trip for him, with all the changes and all the people. He doesn't like change. We did the best we could to prepare, but it's still strange and new.

"Fergus?" I say again. "Are you okay?"

He doesn't answer. He frowns and taps faster.

"Fergus?" I repeat.

"He's fine," Grandfather snaps. "Don't smother the boy. He'll come along when we go. We won't leave him."

My cheeks go hot like I've been slapped. I wasn't *smothering*. That's my *job*. I try to catch Fergus's eye, to make sure he's all right, but he's still staring at his feet. Grandfather jerks his chin forward, and I follow the tug of Grandmother's arm into the middle of the busy, bright, loud airport, Fergus trailing behind us. I keep looking back to make sure he's there, that he's really okay.

I'm not sure this is going to work out after all.

Fergus

I've decided Grandfather is navy blue. Even his voice sounds navy blue, a dark, strict color with no room for cheerful yellow or green. Grandmother is pink, the color of the inside of Mom's jewelry box. I like to touch that sometimes, the satin. It's smooth and slippery. I imagine myself touching it now, silky under my fingers.

"Pink and blue," I say aloud, to taste the words. "Blue and pink."

I feel Grandfather's eyes on me, but I look out the window. We're in a black cab, crawling through London traffic. There are so many cars, lines of red lights keeping us from moving. At least we're crawling closer to the city now, so the buildings are getting interesting. Even though lots of them look almost the same—tan and brown, and red brick, red brick, red brick—each one has a story. Hundreds of years of history. Or thousands. I read that London was founded in 1000 BC by a Greek, Brutus of Troy, when he slayed the giant Gogmagog. I think that's the best name I've ever seen. Gogmagog. The book said it probably comes from people not being able to say Gawr Madoc, a Welsh name that means Madoc the Great.

I can imagine a whole story about Madoc the Great, Gogmagog, tramping through the fields long ago, his giant feet leaving marks in the mud. Maybe right where we are! I laugh and clap my hands, picturing it.

"Fergus," Grandfather says in his navy-blue voice, "what would you like to visit while you're here?"

I don't answer because the question is too big, with too many possibilities. I look at the clouds out the window. Gray. It might rain. It rains a lot here, even in the summer. We looked up the weather on the computer at home so I'd know what to expect. I like rain. It doesn't rain a lot at home, but when it does, I like to go out in it, let it drip over me. It feels as if I'm connecting directly with nature, with the water cycle.

I slip my mini voice recorder out of my pocket and

press Record. Sometimes I listen to conversations later and figure out what people really meant, when I have more time to think about it. Or sometimes I just like to listen to them talk. Especially Mom.

This recorder is old. It was Dad's—he used it in his job as a reporter. Mom said she found it in a drawer after he died, when I was a baby. You can hold it in your hand, small and silver, with a button on the side that's smooth. No one even knows I have the voice recorder, most of the time. Mom likes that I use it. Full circle, she says.

"The British Museum, for sure," Clover says. "We talked a lot about that. Isn't it near your house?"

"It is," Grandfather answers. "Very close, a few minutes' walk." He clears his throat. "But I asked Fergus. What would you most like to see at the British Museum, Fergus?"

I focus hard on the question, because I can tell he's one of those people who really wants answers. It's a smaller question anyway. The British Museum. I studied the website for a long time and looked at images of everything, so I can picture it in my head.

"I want to see the Greek and Roman rooms," I say. Grandmother flinches next to me, so maybe I was loud. "Greek and Roman," I say again, quieter.

"Excellent," Grandfather says. "I know—"

"There's a spear-butt dedicated to Zeus," I add, before I can forget. "And an ax dedicated to Hera. I want to see those. Also, the pediments from the Parthenon. And there's a vase with Hermes. Probably lots of things with Hermes. Hermes is my favorite."

I tell them all about Hermes. He had winged feet that he could use to fly, and a staff that made people fall asleep. He killed a giant, too. More than one. Hippolytus and then Argus.

Talking about Hermes is relaxing and exciting at the same time. I know so much about him that it's easy to feel good talking about it. I'm glad Grandfather asked.

The buildings outside get different, closer together. There are roses above some of the windows, and I see a big white building that looks like it came from Greece. We stop and start a lot, as the driver zooms between cars. I don't like that—the jerking or the rushing between cars. It's too fast, too sudden. I keep talking so I don't have to think about it. I tell them about *Clash of the Titans,* my favorite movie, with Zeus and Hera and Thetis and the hero, Perseus.

After a while we turn next to a green park and stop in front of a tall house on the corner. Number fourteen.

"We're here!" Grandmother says. "Welcome to our home."

I stop the recording. We slide out and stare up at the house. It looks familiar, but that's because I looked at it on the computer, with Mom. She had Grandmother and Grandfather send some pictures, too, of the outside and the inside, all the rooms, so I'd know what to expect. I lean my head back far. I can see six stories from here, including one that's down below street level, and a big attic window at the top. It's all tan brick, with peach-colored brick around the windows, and iron railings, all different sizes, on the first three levels. A black drainpipe slithers down the side. The front door is double, big and black, with a curved window above it and the peach-colored stone curving above that.

It's fancy.

"It was built in 1808," Grandmother says behind me, her voice bright pink. "It's a perfect example of Georgian architecture. My family has been here since the 1830s. Of course, we took the whole house then, servants' quarters and all. Now we just have the top two floors." She winks. "We had to keep the attic."

Clover touches my arm, so I look at her. She's smiling big. "It's so *pretty*, isn't it?"

"It's so pretty," I echo.

My head feels foggy, the tiredness of not sleeping and the time difference between here and home clouding it. We got on the plane at nine p.m. in San Diego—

bedtime—but it's past five p.m. now, and we didn't sleep much on the way here.

I don't know if I think the house is pretty or not, but I hope it has a nice bed.

We have our own room in the attic, which Grandmother says used to be the nursery. She winked again when she said that, but I don't know why. I follow my feet slowly up the narrow stairs, and Grandmother opens a tall white door. "Here you are!" she says. "I hope you love it."

It looks like the pictures, but smaller when you see it all at once. There are two big beds, one on each side of the room, with fluffy white bedspreads. A dark wood floor stretches between them, and a sloped ceiling that I want to touch, to run my fingers along as far as I can reach. A big window sits evenly between the beds, bigger than me, with giant shutters and a bench underneath you can sit on, and white curtains. In the corner there's a dollhouse, a rocking horse that's too small to ride, and a shelf of books. The room looks old, and not like anything I know. But it feels warm and welcoming. Like it wants us to be here.

"Oh!" Clover squeaks. "It's beautiful! Mom grew up here?"

"Not just your mother," Grandmother says. "I did too. And your great-grandmother before that. And her mother." She rests a hand on my shoulder, and I want to squirm away—I don't like being touched like that—but I just step forward into the room, reaching up to touch the ceiling. The wood is smooth, like I hoped. I go to the window and look out at the green square, the red and brown buildings rising around it. I like this window. I want to sit here tomorrow, just sit and look at the city spread out like a map.

Clover's stomach growls, and Grandmother laughs. "Yes. I did promise dinner. Come on, and then you can rest."

We eat dinner—cheese pizza, which I nibble at even though the cheese is wrong, too thick and too sharp—and I make it through without having to say anything. Grandmother keeps smiling at us. Grandfather I don't really look at yet. There's something about him that bothers me. It's the way he looks at me, I think, like he's disapproving. After dinner we call Mom. Clover chatters to her about the plane and the house and lots of things. I say hi.

I get more and more tired, until my head feels like it's going to float away. Finally Grandmother tells us to go up to our room and go to bed if we want. Even though it's light outside, it's late enough, she says. Jet lag shouldn't be too bad.

When we get back to the nursery, I only get as far as the doorway. I'm too tired to take another step. Everything feels fuzzy, blurry.

Clover goes to the window. She gazes out at the green square and London and asks me to do something. Look outside, I think.

I'm too tired for even that. I feel everything hit me at once: the plane, the people, the airport, all the voices and bright lights, no sleep, all the changes, all the holding everything in when I wanted to be feeling things and shouting loud. So many new things. So, so many hours of concentrating and talking and paying attention when I just wanted to be by myself. At home. In our room, in my own bed, where I know what everything will be like. Here it's the wrong food, wrong sounds, wrong textures, wrong people. *Wrong*.

"Wrong," I whisper. "Wrong wrong wrong."

I think I need to scream, to let out the pressure in my head, the *too much*. I want to hold it in. I don't want to do this the first night. But I don't think I can stop it. I feel like my body is going to explode if I don't scream, and I can't. . . .

I drop to the floor, hug my legs, and close my eyes.

It helps to get small. To rock in my own rhythm. Not the world's.

"Fergus, are you all right?"

I hear Clover dimly, but I can't reply. I rock, keeping my eyes shut tight, the floor hard against my tailbone, which already hurts from the plane. I moan a little, the rhythm the same as the rocking. My chest aches, stretching, like something inside is trying to escape. The moan changes slowly into a scream, the way a siren can't help getting louder. It feels bad—I know I shouldn't scream, not here—but good at the same time, to be letting it out. It helps the *too much* pressure.

"It's okay," Clover says somewhere near me. "It's okay, whatever you need to do. But I'm going to sing, okay? I'm just going to sing, and you can listen if you want."

There's knocking behind me. I rock, and keep screaming. Let it out, all of it. Let the wrongness go. That's what Mom says. *Let the wrongness go.*

"Be right back," Clover says. I feel her absence, a space of cold air, and hear voices. They're too harsh, they're *wrong,* and I feel worse, like I might spin off into blackness. Then she's back, not touching me, but sitting right next to me, solid.

"Alouette, gentille alouette," she starts, low.

Clover's voice is like water, calm blue ocean water circling me, soothing me. I listen to it. The scream gets a little quieter, the siren dying down to a moan again, so I can hear.

"Alouette, je te plumerai. . . ."

I focus on her voice, picture that ocean. A Greek ocean like I've seen in books, so clear, a magical, bright blue. The ocean Odysseus sailed through.

"Alouette, gentille alouette. Alouette, je te plumerai."

The moan stops, and my breath starts to come back to normal. The pressure is almost gone. I like this song. Weirdly, it's about plucking the feathers off a bird, in French.

"Je te plumerai la tête, je te plumerai la tête. Et la tête, et la tête! Alouette! Alouette! Ohhhh . . ."

I open my eyes. I see Clover right next to me, watching the floor as she sings, her hands folded, a line in the middle of her forehead, like Mom's.

Behind her, at the window, I see a boy.

He's about my age, dressed all in green. He has reddish hair that curls wildly like mine, pink cheeks, thick eyebrows, and a pointed nose. He's floating there in the window, watching us. Floating outside a sixth-story window.

He waves one hand and smiles at me. He has strange

baby teeth, with too much gum showing, but I still want to smile back. To *grin* back.

"Clover," I whisper so she'll see him too. But before the word is out of my mouth, he turns and flies away. In a second he's out of sight, like he was never there.

Clover stops singing. She sits back on her heels. "Are you feeling better?"

I shut my eyes tight again. I don't want to tell her about the boy. It would be too hard to find the words, to even try to explain whatever just happened. Besides, he left when I tried to show her. Maybe he came for *me*. I like that thought.

I think I'll keep that secret to myself.

Clover

I wake up in the middle of the night and can't go to sleep again for a couple of hours. I stay in bed anyway, watching the curtains sway in the breeze from the open window. The lights of London aren't visible from the bed, but it feels *different* from home. I hope we can have fun here. I hope that I'm wrong about Grandfather and that Mom gets all her studying done and passes the bar exam. She could be a lawyer soon! That's exciting.

I hope that I do my job well and Fergus makes it through this trip okay. I have to be his person, since Mom's not here.

Sometimes—almost always at night—I wish that

everything could be *easier*. I wish that Fergus didn't have to struggle so much. That Mom was home more. That Dad hadn't died. I wish I could stay after school and do choir instead of hurrying home. I always have to be there.

But I can't stop my brain from worrying about Fergus, about Mom, about school, about things I know are silly. In daylight I don't allow those thoughts to get through. I don't want to be that kind of person. I want to be calm, and sure, and able to handle anything.

I glance over at Fergus—snoring gently—close my eyes, and hum songs until I go back to sleep.

In the morning we go downstairs to the main apartment, where Grandmother and Grandfather live. It's beautiful, with gold light pouring in the windows onto flowered peach wallpaper and heavy, dark furniture. It looks like one of those British PBS shows Mom watches. Everything feels historical and plush and, well, *nice*. Not like our flea-market furniture at home. I try to imagine Mom here as a little girl, as a teenager, but I can't. She doesn't fit.

Do I fit? Mom always says I'm just like her. Maybe that's why I feel strange here.

At the bottom of the stairs the wall is packed with old pictures, mostly black-and-white. There are even a few that are paintings, not photographs. I stop to look, and Fergus waits a few feet away. I lean in close to get a better look at a picture of a girl dressed in white, her hair down her back. She's staring off into the distance, with a secret smile. She looks a little like Mom, I think, like me. The picture next to it is of the same girl with two boys, both younger than her, in old-fashioned suits, their arms around each other. Her brothers, probably.

"Do you think they're our relatives?" I ask.

"Every last one." Grandmother pokes her head around the corner, her eyes crinkling up. Her hair's in a long braid today. She points at the picture of the three together. "That one has a special and wonderful story. But come and have breakfast. I'll introduce you to them later."

We follow her around the corner to a little kitchen tucked in the back of the house. There's a gleaming black stove taking up most of the space, almost bigger than the refrigerator next to it. Fergus runs a finger along the counter, a smooth, swirled marble. He leans down really close to it so he can see the pattern. I nod to Grandfather, who's reading the newspaper at a round table. He nods back. It smells good in here, like the ghost of bacon.

"Is this the original kitchen?" I ask.

Grandmother laughs. "Oh, no. The original kitchen was most of the bottom floor. With the poor servants having to run all the way up the back stairs with food trays. A lovely young man lives there now who teaches literature at the university. He visits us sometimes, for inspiration. Sit, sit. Fergus—your mother says you like buttered toast in triangles, yes? Clover, would you like eggs? Fried?"

"I'll have toast too, please," I say. "I always feel like fried eggs are looking at me."

Grandfather snorts. Grandmother bustles around, getting breakfast. I check on Fergus. He seems all right, standing there looking at the kitchen, at the flowered wallpaper, running his finger back and forth along the counter. I sit next to Grandfather. He glances at me over the paper but keeps reading.

This is awkward. I don't know how to start a conversation, or even if I should. I stare at the table, looking at all the little scratches and dents and rings. This table must have been here for a long time. Everything in this house feels old, worn . . . but in a good way. Worn by our family. It's weird that we've never been here before.

I really want to talk to Mom, to ask questions about all of this, about growing up here. When we talked to her last night, her voice sounded so far away and small. With the time difference, she's asleep now.

"Jack," Grandmother says, spreading butter on thick toast, "ask them."

Grandfather clears his throat and lays down his paper. "Would you two like to visit the British Museum with me this morning?"

Fergus starts to rock back and forth on his heels, his hands fluttering around his face. *Flying,* he calls that. "British Museum," he says, low. "British Museum."

I smile. "Yes," I say. "Thank you. That's a definite yes."

"How do you know?" Grandfather asks.

I frown. "How do I know what?"

Grandfather points at Fergus, who's still rocking, looking at the wall. "How do you know he wants to go? He didn't *say* yes." His face is so serious, I can't tell if he's really interested or mocking.

I bite my lip. I have to assume he's interested. "His hands do that when he's excited about something, or happy," I say. "Rocking can mean he's either upset or excited, but if you pair it with the hands, and repeating the words, he's telling us yes."

Grandfather grunts. "But why doesn't he just say yes? He can speak normally."

"Jack," Grandmother interrupts. "Enough." She sets two plates of buttered toast, cut in perfect triangles, on the table. "The museum it is, then," she says cheerfully. "After you get back, I can introduce you to your illustrious relatives." She smiles, looking so much like Mom that it startles me for a moment. I rub my finger over a dent in the table as Fergus sits next to me and eats his toast.

I take a deep breath and let it out slowly. It's all okay. Everything will be okay, even without Mom. The British Museum is a great start . . . even with Grandfather.

I see what Mom meant about Grandfather when she was talking to Great-Aunt Tilly and didn't think I heard. Cold and distant, she said. He doesn't listen to anyone. That's why she left, why she never came back.

I glance at him again and take a bite of my toast. It'll all be okay. It'll be fine.

The best thing about this neighborhood is that it's on a square: that's what it's called, and all the houses are built in an actual square around a massive park in the center, an iron fence barely holding in the explosion of green. Grandmother and Grandfather's house is on the corner, directly across from the open gate. We stand on their steps and look at the park. There's a little green building just outside the fence, a café. The sun is warm and bright, lighting up the trees like a fairyland. It looks different from the parks in San Diego, with unfamiliar tall, leafy trees instead of eucalyptus, but the feeling is the same. It seems green and calm, a place to escape to.

I turn around to ask Grandfather about it—how old it is, whether those are the original trees—but I don't even get the words out before he swears loudly, and I jump.

"So sorry," he says immediately. "It's only . . . does that boy ever do what he's meant to?"

I spin back just in time to see Fergus disappear into the park.

Oh, I should've known he'd do that. It's so *tempting*. I kind of wanted to go explore it myself. I wouldn't, of course, because we're supposed to go to the museum. But I wanted to.

"I'll go get him," I say, and run down the steps. "Be right back."

I think I hear swearing again behind me, but I don't look. I have to find Fergus and get us back on track for the morning.

I trot through the open iron gate. A small group of trees and plants is in front when you come in, and a path that goes right and left on either side of it. There are actually far fewer trees in here than I thought, once you're inside. On the other side of the group of trees, another path heads toward the middle. Surprisingly, there are a lot of people in here, walking through, lounging on the grass, sitting on the benches. I shade my eyes and squint in all directions, trying to spot Fergus's rumpled head in the middle of all the people. I don't see him. I have to find him. Do I go left, right, or straight?

I remember Fergus saying that in the old mazes, you always go right. I run to the right, past dark bushes sprinkled with little white flowers that smell sweet. I keep going, looking everywhere. When I get to the other corner with no Fergus, I take one of the middle paths, to the center of the park. There's a fountain, with benches circling it. It's oddly flat, with a grate all the way around to drain it, and jets of water bubbling up all over. Children squat in the shallow water, their hands over the jets, laughing. Fat pigeons waddle past. Busy people with headphones walk through, drinking coffee.

No Fergus.

I thought for sure he'd come to the middle, to the fountain. I don't see Grandfather, either—maybe he didn't follow us in. I frown, feeling a little sick. I'm not doing very well at taking care of Fergus. Five minutes into the first day and I already lost him.

4

Fergus

I follow the ball of light through the trees, past all the people. I'm supposed to be somewhere else, I know that, but I couldn't help it. The little light danced right in front of the gate, twisting in the air like a live, bright leaf, and when it flew into the park, I had to follow it. I had to see how it could move like that.

It could be a spark, or some strangely lit piece of fluff. But it looks like a will-o'-the-wisp.

In folklore, will-o'-the-wisps are floating lights that lead travelers where they're not supposed to go, like bogs or quicksand. They're called Hessdalen lights in Norway, and Martebo lights in Sweden. In the movie

Brave they're spirits who help people. I'm not worried about following this one. It's a park, so even if it was the bad kind of spirit, there isn't a bog or anything I could fall into.

I almost crash into a man jogging the other way, and he looks at me squinty-eyed. He doesn't look at the light, though. I wonder if he even notices the light, if anyone else does.

It *is* small, but it seems obvious to me.

The smell of the park surrounds me, earth and trees and flowers, so strong I can taste it in the back of my throat. The path stretches ahead through an arcade with thin trees bending over it, following an iron arch. There aren't any people on this part of the path, so I can focus on the ball of light, zipping away too fast down the lane of trees. I run, my hands flying.

The light stops suddenly, and I catch up to it hovering in front of a little birdhouse attached to one of the trees. The house is brightly painted with flowers, and I realize the hole is too big for it to be a birdhouse— it's more like a message box. The sign says OPEN ME! CONTINUE THE STORY. The light ball dances in front of my face, and I reach out, not quite touching it. It's warm, like a candle. Definitely not a spark or fluff. The light is searing so close to my eyes. I squeeze them shut.

The warmth fades away. When I open my eyes again, the light ball has left the path of trees, hovering next to a clump of dark green bushes with drooping pink flowers. Fuchsia.

"Don't go!" I say. "Don't go."

It flies around the corner and I run after it, behind another café with empty tables out front. It's deserted back here, hidden from the rest of the park.

A face peeks around the edge of a thick tree, and I squeak. It's the boy. The same boy from last night, with the red hair and the pointy nose, studying me. The light ball dances by his cheek, making his green eyes glow. He stands slowly, the light moving with him, and waves hello, like last night.

"Hello," I say, so quietly I almost can't hear myself.

"Fergus! There you are!" Clover yells from behind me. "Fergus!"

I turn reluctantly.

She's panting, and her cheeks are red. "I couldn't find you! Why'd you run off like that?"

I point to the boy and the light. But when I turn back to look, they're gone. There's nothing there.

I run to the tree as fast as I can. Nothing. I see only bushes and fence, and the cars rushing by outside the park. There's nothing down the path but a trash can and a few regular people.

"Fergus?" Clover asks. "Are you okay?"

"The boy," I say. "The boy from the window was here. And a ball of light."

Clover frowns. "What are you talking about? Come on—we have to get back. Grandfather is waiting for us."

"A ball of light," I say, the words tumbling over each other. "A ball of light, dancing right in front of me."

She stares at me for a second, then shakes her head. "One of your myths? Come on. We have to *go*."

"No!" I yell loudly. She's not listening to me. She always does this. If she would just *listen*, I could tell her about the boy and the light, and then maybe they would come back. They left when she came, both times. But if she understood what I saw, maybe she could see them too.

She sighs, her arms folded. "Fergus—"

"No!" I repeat. "*Listen*. Listen listen listen."

She tilts her head but doesn't interrupt again. I can tell this is going to be hard to describe in words. But I'm going to have to try.

I finally get Clover to understand about the boy from last night—she gets mad that I didn't tell her before, and I get mad that she doesn't believe me at first—but after we finish being mad, I get the words out so they make sense to her. I tell her about the light ball too, though that's difficult to explain. Well, the boy floating at the window is difficult to explain too, but I think Clover believes I saw him.

"We need to tell Grandmother and Grandfather about it," she says. She always wants to tell grown-ups right away, whenever anything happens. We're sitting on the path by the clump of bushes, away from everyone. I pluck one of the glossy leaves and feel it with my thumb.

I want to wait to see what the boy wants before I tell anyone else. He's clearly coming to see *me,* and it doesn't feel like something for grown-ups. I quote from *Clash of the Titans.* " 'Oh impetuous . . . foolish . . . Ah dear, the young. Why do they never listen? When will they ever learn?' "

She frowns again. "*Titans?*"

I nod.

"You mean they're not going to believe us," she says.

"Believe *me,*" I say. The leaf feels smooth, though I accidentally prick my thumb on a thorn on the edge.

"They're not going to believe you," she echoes.

"Right. You're probably right. But . . . if he was staring in our window, no matter how he got there, that's creepy and we need to tell someone. Especially since he was here again today, hiding from people. It's suspicious." Her forehead does the Mom lines. "He might have been trying to lure you away somewhere."

If she saw him, she wouldn't think he was suspicious. I know, deep down, that he's not someone to be scared of. But I also think she's not going to change her mind. She never changes her mind, and there's not much I can say to budge her, like always. I shrug, and she stands up.

"Let's go back to Grandfather," she says. "We still get to go to the museum, and then we'll tell them after."

I make Clover let me explore the fountain in the middle of the park before we leave. I run the last bit when I see it—I didn't really look at it before. It doesn't have a pool or anything, only jets shooting up out of a flat circle in the ground. I step right over to one of the jets and put my hands in it, bubbly water pushing up under my fingers, then pouring over, cool and trickly. There are a lot of people, kids laughing and grown-ups talking and pigeons cooing, but I tune it all out and focus on the water, the sun making patterns of light. I always like looking at water, and feeling it at the same time is even better. I could just stay here.

After a while, Clover tells me we *really* have to leave if we're going to get to the British Museum. I remember the Hermes vase and the Zeus spear and the Parthenon room, and I get excited again. It's okay to leave the water for that.

When we come out of the park, though, Grandfather isn't there.

Clover stops and looks around, at the steps and the entrance and the little green building on the corner, but he's just not there.

"I guess he got tired of waiting," she says. "We did take a long time." I follow her across the street and up the steps again, all the way back up to the apartment. It's a lot of stairs. But when we get there, Grandmother is alone, sitting in a flowered chair, a cup of tea steaming in front of her on the table.

She looks at us sadly. "No British Museum today? Grandfather said you clearly didn't want to go right now, so perhaps another day."

I feel the pressure in my head. We were supposed to go *today*.

Clover sits on the sofa. "Where is Grandfather?" she asks quietly. "Is he angry?"

Grandmother shrugs. "He went for a walk on his own. And he's a bit upset, probably. It's important to him that things go according to plan. Your mother in-herited that from him." She looks at us, and her face softens. "He'll recover—don't worry."

I tap my fingers on my leg. Grandfather's angry on the first day, because of me. "Ball of light," I whisper, to remember why I went into the park, why it was important. "Ball of light. And the boy."

Grandmother looks up sharply. "The boy?" She looks at me, then at Clover. "What boy?"

I move to the window. I can see the city from here, a different view than the square. I didn't mean to tell her like that. I didn't mean to say it out loud.

"Fergus saw a boy last night at our window," Clover says slowly. "Um . . . floating outside our window. And then he saw the boy again today in the park. And a . . . flying ball of light . . ."

She sounds unsure. I tap on my leg, humming. I know they won't believe me. They'll say I'm crazy. I hate it when people say that.

But Grandmother gasps. "A pixie! And Peter. Oh, he's back."

I turn around. She knows who he is.

"Peter? And a *pixie*?" Clover asks.

"Indeed," Grandmother says. "Come with me. I have such a wonderful story to tell you both."

Clover

Grandmother reaches out a hand, her eyes bright, and I take it. Her hand is warm. She takes me to the wall of pictures by the stairs, Fergus right behind. I see him slip his voice recorder out of his pocket and hit the button.

"Have either of you read the story of Peter Pan?" Grandmother's voice softens. "Did your mother read it to you?"

"I have," I say. "From the library at school. But Mom got mad when she saw the book, and told me to return it. I'd already finished anyway."

Grandmother sighs. "Fergus? Did you read it?" He shakes his head. "Or perhaps you've seen the movie?"

"It's a Disney movie," Fergus says. "I've seen it four times."

She nods and clasps her hands together. "Then we have somewhere to start. That story, my dear ones, is true, roughly." She smiles. "Wendy Darling was my grandmother, your great-great-grandmother. That's her there, in the white dress." I lean in again to the picture of the girl with the secret smile. She does look like Mom. That's Wendy?

"This picture, now . . ." She points to the next one. "That is Wendy with her brothers. Wendy, John, and Michael. And this house"—she points up the stairs, toward our attic—"is where it all started, in your nursery. Your grandfather doesn't accept any of this. I tried to tell him about Peter once, but he wouldn't believe it. But when I was your age, Peter came to that window and took me on a trip to Neverland." She gazes up the stairs dreamily, like she's there now.

Wait, Peter Pan is *real*?

"Neverland," Fergus repeats. "Neverland. Neverland is real." His forehead wrinkles. "Neverland is not real. It's a story."

"Oh, but it is real. It's a wonderful place—terrible, mind, but wonderful, too—created partly by the imaginations of the children who go there, so it's different for everyone. I remember so much. . . ." She sighs again, a little huff. "No." She shakes her head. "This is not about my time in Neverland. This is about yours. When Peter brought Wendy home, he promised that he'd come back sometimes to take her for a visit for a week or two. It's even at the end of the book. He carried that on with my mother, Jane, and then with me."

"And Mom?" I ask, disbelieving. "Did Mom go to Neverland and never tell us?"

"No." She shrugs, and her face goes sad again. "Your mother never went, as far as I know. Your mother is very . . . based in the real world, like her father. She claimed not to believe in it, in Peter." She shakes her head, her eyes wide. "How could you not believe, when it is true?"

"Neverland," Fergus says. "I want to go to Neverland."

I look at him, astonished. Usually it's hard for him to change, or to try new things. It took an awful lot of planning, detailing and mapping everything, before he would feel comfortable coming here. I was even a little surprised he slept in a strange bed okay last night. But he wants to go to a mythical land? Without any maps or guidebooks?

Seriously?

"And so you can, it seems," Grandmother continues.

"That was Peter last night, of course. And this morning. And that ball of light? That was a pixie. J. M. Barrie called them 'fairies' in the book, but they prefer 'pixies.'" She smiles at us. "Peter's back to take you on an adventure. If you leave the window open tonight, he'll come in. And you can go."

I stare at the picture again, my brain whirling. We can *go*? Tonight?

Grandmother rests a hand on my shoulder. "You *can* go. It's all right. Peter will watch out for you, and he'll bring you back before too long. He's done it with us all, except your mother." She smiles again, a small and secret smile like Wendy's. "It's a family tradition."

Fergus runs to the window, looking out at the city. "It's a story. We can go into a *story*."

My chest tightens. I don't know if I want to go to Neverland. Wonderful . . . but terrible, she said. In the book there were pirates and wild animals, poison and jealous pixies. It was so unpredictable and scary. How could we possibly be safe there?

And Mom didn't go. Shouldn't I be like Mom?

But Fergus seems to want to go. Maybe because it's like one of his myths. I think Peter came for Fergus today, not me. He ran away when I came. He wants to take *Fergus* on an adventure.

Of course, if Fergus really wants to go, I'll have to go with him. I have to protect him.

I don't like this at all.

Grandmother gives us a book to look at "very carefully," a first edition of *Peter and Wendy*. It's not the first book that Peter Pan appeared in, but it's the one with the story we all know, with Wendy and John and Michael going to Neverland. The book is heavy, green-brown with gold foil stamped on the front.

Fergus and I lie next to each other on the floor of the nursery and open the book.

I touch the inscription. "It *is* true."

In sloppy, scrawled handwriting it says *To my own Darlings. With kindest regards, J. M. Barrie.*

Fergus wrinkles his nose. "It smells. Like the used-book store with the cats."

I laugh. It does.

"But Wendy is *real*," I say. "And she's our great-great-grandmother. It's so . . . weird. Why didn't Mom tell us?"

It feels like Mom was lying, not telling us a secret that big.

Fergus turns the pages and stops at a black-and-white illustration that says *The Never Never Land*. A boy dressed in green leaves is playing on a pipe, with wolves and a crocodile near him, and a whole line of pirates. In the background there's a lagoon and a big pirate ship. Even in the drawing you can tell it's a wild place, with tall mountains and jungle and animals everywhere.

"The boy," Fergus says. "It's the boy." He touches it gently.

I turn to the next illustration, *Peter Flew In*. It doesn't look exactly like our attic, but close. Peter is standing in the window, and three children are sleeping in their beds. Ahead of Peter, on the floor, is a fairy—or pixie, Grandmother said—who fills the room with light. It really does look just like a glowing ball. You can't see anything else. "Is that what it looked like?" I ask. "The pixie?"

"Pixie," Fergus says. His hands fly up around his face. "A ball of light, dancing."

I shiver, suddenly cold. Pixies. In the book, Tinker Bell gets jealous and tries to kill Wendy. Wendy, who's my great-great-grandmother. Do we really want to go to a place like that? What if the pixies are still jealous?

It sounds dangerous.

I flip almost to the end of the book, peering at the text. "In the book," I say, "the pirates all died or left.

So maybe there aren't pirates now?" I turn the page, and we both lean over a picture called *Peter and Jane*. It's the nursery-attic again, with Wendy as a woman, her hair up, and another little girl flying high in the air, her pigtails floating behind her.

"That's our great-grandmother," I say. I read the last paragraph out loud.

" 'Jane is now a common grown-up, with a daughter called Margaret; and every spring-cleaning time, except when he forgets, Peter comes for Margaret and takes her to the Neverland, where she tells him stories about himself, to which he listens eagerly. When Margaret grows up she will have a daughter, who is to be Peter's mother in turn; and thus it will go on, so long as children are gay and innocent and heartless.' "

"Margaret is Grandmother," I say. "And that was supposed to be Mom, the last one. But she didn't go."

Why didn't Mom ever go? Was she scared? Or was she smart, to stay safe at home? Should I be like Mom, who stayed home, or like Wendy, who went with Peter to Neverland?

"I want to go," Fergus says firmly. He puts his hand flat across the page. "Peter Pan." Then he frowns. "Pan. Like Hermes's son." He sits back on his heels, his words coming faster. "Peter is like one of the gods, immortal.

He comes to the world only when he wants to. He's like Hermes. They both fly. They're both mischievous and get in trouble a lot."

His face lights up. "What if . . . Peter is really Hermes's son Pan? He supposedly died, but you never know with gods. In that first picture, Peter is even playing Pan's pipe. What if he really is one of the Greek gods, hiding in Neverland?"

He jumps up, digs in his bag, and pulls out the *Dictionary of Mythology*, eagerly scanning the pages.

"You really do want to go," I say from the floor. He doesn't answer, but it's obvious he does. So it doesn't matter that Mom didn't go, or that I'm scared. I know without any doubt: we're going to Neverland.

It would be nice if Grandmother and Grandfather had a big dog like Nana in the original book. A dog hug would help me feel less afraid, I think. And less alone.

But if I'm going to Neverland, I have to be brave. I have to be like Wendy.

Fergus

It's too late to be up, eleven o'clock. Normally, Clover insists we be in bed by nine, even when Mom is working or studying late. She's stricter about it than Mom. But here we are, awake. Waiting for Peter Pan.

I hope he comes.

We left one lamp on in our room, by Clover's bed, but it only makes the rest of the room look dark: black holes of shadow that might suck you in if you went too close. A breeze blows through sometimes and makes the curtains swirl. It startles me every time.

The window is wide open. Clover and I are sitting on our beds, fully dressed—Clover said she wasn't going on an adventure in her pj's, and I don't care what she wears. I'm wearing my soft Tardis shirt and my most comfy shorts, with no tags. She's wearing her bright blue shirt, her hair in a bun on top of her head like usual. She made us pack our backpacks with things she thought we might need: extra clothes and underwear, our toothbrushes, towels. Grandmother said we shouldn't bring anything, because "that's not the point of Neverland," but Clover said if she was going, she was going to be prepared.

I'm bringing two of my mythology books because I would feel strange if they were here and I was far away. I like to have them with me. What if I want to look something up? I definitely will want to look things up. I also have my voice recorder, in my pocket. I can play my recordings of Mom if I want, or of Clover singing. Or of Grandmother telling the story of Peter. And I can record things . . . sounds in Neverland. Even Peter, maybe. Or pixies, if they make noise.

If it really happens. We've been waiting a long time. Maybe he's not coming back. I tap my fingers, the rhythm soothing, easing the worry in my mind.

I asked Grandmother all about what Neverland was like, but she said it's different for everyone. She loved horses when she was little, so she had an adventure saving a wild horse from a dragon. She says you can't plan for it. I wish I could, though. I like to know what's going to happen, and what a place looks like. I like to know what I'm going to be expected to do.

What am I going to be expected to do?

"Clover," I whisper. "It'll be okay, won't it?"

Her eyes shine in the lamplight. She's sitting stiffly on the edge of her bed, her feet flat on the floor. "I hope so. Grandmother will explain to Mom, after we're gone, and Grandfather. And we'll be back soon, she said. It'll be okay."

"I can see we need to teach you about the Neverland."

I gasp. Peter stands in the window, one hand braced on the top, like the illustration in the book. He's wearing clothes made of brown cloth, not leaves like in the picture. He leaps softly into the room. A light follows him, the size of my little finger, then another bigger one, zipping around his head, and another. Light blooms out from them. "Pixies," I say under my breath. I'm glad I know now what they are.

Peter stands between us, arms crossed, legs spread wide. "We do not," he says sternly, "go to the Neverland worrying about parents or when we will come back." His voice is high, but it doesn't bother me like high voices sometimes do. It fits him. "I will not have that kind of talk. If you go to the Neverland, you go for fun. Adventure. Freedom. Will you go?" He looks at Clover, then at me, and it feels like he's judging us.

Then he flings his arms out wide and he laughs, loud. "Of course you'll go. We will have such a marvelous time. It has been long and long since we had a Wendy to mother us."

"I'm Clover," my sister says sharply. "Not Wendy. I'm not going to *mother* anyone."

One of the lights dives toward her and hovers in front of her face. She squints but doesn't move. That's her sour face. I recognize it.

Peter raises his eyebrows. "But you will sing for us, yes? Your singing brought me here last night. Better than the mermaids, though don't tell them I said so. And you are a fine mother, I think."

He looks at me. I squirm, feeling like I should do something, say something. I don't know what I should do. I look down. "Pan," I whisper. "Hermes and Pan." One of the other lights comes close to my face, and I shut my eyes against the brightness. I wish I could see the pixie instead of just the light. It's warm, though, like before.

"You," Peter says slowly, "are not a John. You are a Lost Boy."

I open my eyes, and the pixie darts away. "I am Fergus."

"Just so. You are Fergus. And *I* am Peter Pan." He grins, showing his small teeth, and this time I do grin back. I can't help it. Even Clover smiles a little, her sour face melting away.

"Your color is green," I say. I clap my hands. It fits so well. Even his eyes are green. "You're deep green all over, like a forest." I wonder if he is a god, if he is Hermes's son. Do all the gods have colors, like everyone else?

Peter nods. "Of course I am green. I come from the forest and the garden." He frowns. "Your voice . . . both of you. You sound strange. Flat."

"We're American," Clover says.

He shrugs. "You will have to explain 'American.' But you are from Wendy, I feel that."

He tilts his head at Clover. "You will come, won't you? The last Wendy . . ." He makes a funny, tight face. Suddenly he springs up next to Clover on her bed, grabs her hands, and pulls her to her feet. "Jump!" he shouts. He starts bouncing with her on the bed. "Jump! Jump!" He laughs. At first Clover looks nervous, but then she laughs too, a laugh like I haven't heard from her in a long time, loud and free. Her bun bobs up and down.

"Happy thoughts, now," Peter says. He laughs again. "Think of the happiest thing you can."

Clover's face scrunches for a moment, like she's trying to think of something while still bouncing. Then all of a sudden it clears, and she smiles, wide and sunny. Then she sings a long, sweet note, her arms spread wide.

"Now, Nari! Donar! Gla!" Peter cries.

One of the pixie lights buzzes around Clover, from her head to her feet, then the others, and on one of the bounces Clover just doesn't come down. Her feet don't touch the bed. Suddenly she's near the ceiling, floating just like Jane in the book. She looks happy, too, like Jane did. "I'm flying!" she shouts, spinning in the air. "Fergus! I'm flying!"

I jump up on my bed. "Me! My turn! My turn!"

Peter flies over and takes my hands. I don't mind, though his hands feel rough, like tree bark. We bounce and bounce and laugh, and the lights zip around me. "Happy thoughts!" Peter calls, and I'm ready. I had my happy thought ready to go, and I let it fill my head.

I imagine being in the British Museum alone, after hours, all the artifacts surrounding me. It's calm, and quiet, with just enough light to see by, and I can look at the Hermes exhibits as much as I want.

Before I know it, I'm floating near the ceiling too.

I feel so free. Nothing is touching me, nothing holding me down. It's the feeling of spinning, but better. I swoop, and laugh at the air on my face. My hands fly from pure joy, and it makes me go higher.

"Away to Neverland!" Peter calls. Without looking back, he flies straight out the window.

Clover looks at me, then dives down and grabs her backpack.

I fly down and pick mine up too, and wriggle it onto my back. I check to make sure my voice recorder is secure in my pocket.

"We follow the North Star," I say.

Clover smiles. She knows it's from *Clash of the Titans,* when they leave on their adventure. I say it a lot when we're setting off somewhere. To me it means *We're ready. Let's go.* But now we're *really* going out into the stars.

"We follow the North Star!" she repeats. She sings again, a little "la-la-*la*!," and giggles.

We fly after Peter into the night. It's scary when we cross the windowsill, the ground dropping out under us. But one of the pixies does a swoop in front of me, so I try one. Joy bubbles up inside me. This is better than I ever imagined. Flying is even more fun out here, in the night, with the lights shining bright below.

The pixie zips forward, like it's reminding me that I need to keep up with Peter, so I do what it does, pushing with my feet like I'm swimming. There's nothing restricting me. I feel as if I'm swimming in the ocean, letting the waves carry me. Except I won't get salt water in my eyes.

I could fly forever.

Clover hovers next to me, her arms wide, her face squinched up against the wind.

I laugh and do another spin, and we fly on, over the city of London.

7

Clover

I'm worried again.

In the book, it took days to get to Neverland. I remember reading about how they flew on and on and on, and they kept falling asleep and almost crashing into the sea, or almost getting lost going through clouds. I don't know if we can do it. I don't know if *I* can do it. I look at all the lights of London far below. It's beautiful, for sure. But how can we possibly make it so far?

How can we possibly be flying at all? We shouldn't be able to. It goes against all the laws of nature.

I drop a few feet, and before I even have time to

scream, Peter is next to me, his red curls blowing back in the breeze.

"Wendy," he scolds, "your doubt is a poisonous cloud, and it's spreading. You cannot doubt while you are flying. You must think happy thoughts. Believe."

"But it's so far," I whisper, and I drop lower. I see Fergus above me now, shooting this way and that, pixies dancing by his head. He seems fine—happy, even. But the worry spreads in my chest. "Does it really take days and days to get there?"

Peter reaches out and catches my hand. Instantly I feel better, calmer, the tightness loosening a little. His hands are warm. Maybe they're magic.

"It takes as long as it takes," he says with a shrug. "Be here now, instead of worrying about the next part. Look at the view around you." He points to Big Ben, not far away, its big, round face shining bright, and the Thames curving like a snake through the city. "Above you." He points at the stars, which seem so close I could touch them if I tried. "Second star to the right, and straight on till morning." He winks. "There's your clue for how long it takes. Now. You had a lovely happy thought to begin flying—I could see it on your face. Think it again. Let it fill you."

I close my eyes and imagine it again: standing on a

stage with a full choir, singing, the notes coming out perfectly, exactly the way I want them. I'm doing a solo, and it's perfect. The packed crowd cheers wildly, and I bow.

Yes!

Peter lets go of my hand and soars up and up and up, and I follow him easily. I push through a little cloud, cold mist on my face, and laugh, surprised. How many people know what it's like inside a cloud?

We fly on until the city changes to countryside below us, and villages. Everything is quiet, with only a few lights here and there shining in windows. England is so pretty, even at night. I try to think only of that, of singing, of being happy . . . instead of worrying about what's next. We keep on to the towns on the coast, houses piled up on the edge of the rocks. The smell of the ocean sweeps over us like a different kind of wave, seaweed and salt water crashing together, and I relax more. It smells like San Diego, like home.

I stretch out my arms and try a little swoop. Peter joins me, and then Fergus, and we swoop around and over each other like wild dragonflies. We fly for a long, long time over the ocean, until the sun starts to peek through the edge of the sky—and I'm not tired at all, or scared anymore. I'm just there, skimming through the air, free.

When a green island appears through the clouds, Peter points and the pixies dart away from us. I stare down at it, fascinated.

We've come to Neverland.

From the air, the island looks mostly like it did in the illustrations in *Peter and Wendy*. There are two big mountain peaks in the middle with snow dusting the tops like powdered sugar, and two round coves, one on the bottom of the island and one on the side. The water in the coves is pure turquoise. I don't see any pirate ships from up here.

I fly next to Peter, as close to him as I can. "Are there still pirates? Crocodiles? Mermaids?" I feel like I should've asked this before.

He laughs, high, and leans in, his breath tickling my ear. "The mermaids are always there. *My* pirates are long vanquished. Margaret told you that story, yes? Captain Hook is well and truly dead, and the crocodile with him. But who's there now? It depends on you. We'll see." He wiggles his eyebrows and dives down, fast, to the far end of the island away from the coves. As we get closer I can see it's an old forest, packed with trees. Fergus shrieks happily and dives down too, and I can't do anything but follow.

Of course it's only then I start to wonder about how we land.

Peter lands lightly on his feet, in the middle of a clearing covered in long grass, his hands on his hips. Fergus and I pretty much crash. I slam down on my side and roll all the way across the clearing, coming up hard against a big tree.

I lie there panting for a minute, sure I've broken all my bones, before daring to wiggle my fingers and toes.

Surprisingly, I'm fine. "Fergus?" I call. "Are you okay?"

No answer.

"Fergus?" I sit up. He's on his feet next to Peter, bouncing, his hands flying happily. He's okay. Neither of us was shot by an arrow, like Wendy was when she first came here, so that's good. We're both still alive. I close my eyes and breathe pure relief.

Until I hear a growl, close. A terrible low growl that makes me instinctively freeze, my pulse pounding in my ears. The grass rustles, and there's a strange, loud huff of breath.

"Peter?" I squeak. "What is that?"

A second later he's next to me—the next second he has a bow in his hand, an arrow notched in it, ready. I don't know where he got it from. He creeps behind me, his bare feet making no sound. Without looking, he waves for me to get out of the way. I stand and scurry over to Fergus, who's watching, eyes wide.

The growl changes to a yowl, definitely catlike. A big cat. I recognize that sound from trips to the San Diego Zoo. They have a recording of it by the cat exhibit, where you can push a button and play it over and over.

It's a mountain lion.

The lion darts from behind the tree where I was sitting, straight at Peter, and I scream. But Peter backs away in time, the arrow still aimed at the cat.

The cat is huge, easily as big as Peter, its fur the color of sand. It has huge, powerful-looking paws and a swinging tail. And sharp predator teeth it's baring at him.

Peter doesn't look worried at all. "It's all right, then, cat," he croons. He moves left, away from us, and the lion follows him on its big feet. "You do not want to tangle with me, then, do you? I'm surprised the other lions did not tell you about me." He laughs, which stops the cat for a moment, before they move together again.

"No lion has ever beat me, nor bear, neither," he says. "But I do not want to kill you today. I just returned home. I am not of that mind." He stops moving and stares at the cat, hard, then takes one step toward it, arrow still notched. The cat doesn't move; only its whiskers twitch. Peter steps closer again, within striking distance of those claws. I clench my fists. "Now go on. Get you away from here, and we shall do this another day when we are both ready." He stares at the cat, and the cat stares back, neither of them blinking.

Suddenly a ball of light—a pixie—shoots straight down out of the sky and zips around the cat's head. Another comes, and another. The cat shakes its giant head as the three pixies buzz around. It slaps a paw at them, confused.

"Enough," Peter says. The pixies fly to Peter, hovering near him. "Go!" Peter shouts to the cat, pointing to a path that leads toward the mountain. "Go!"

The lion leaps, and I scream again, sure it's going to cut Peter to pieces. Fergus screams too. But the cat flies right past, onto the path and away just like Peter told it to, its yellow tail flicking as it disappears into the brush.

Peter lowers the arrow and turns around. "I have not ever seen that kind of cat. You must've brought him with you." The pixies skitter around his head. "Yes. Nari, Donar, Gla. You *did* help. Very well done. Oh, hello, Lost Boys. I've brought one of you, and a new mother."

I spin, and behind Fergus and me, in a tight group, are six kids, our age or younger. Boys and girls both, all wearing dirty, scraggly clothes, their hair wild, staring at us.

"Hello," one of the boys says, a boy with dark skin and curly brown hair.

"Hello," Fergus echoes.

I nod, not sure what to say. Though I want to say what I keep telling Peter. I'm not anyone's mother. Just Clover.

I don't want them to expect Wendy and get me.

Fergus

Even with the sun not all the way up, Neverland is bright. All the colors are more intense than at home, or in London. The grass is a deep jewel green, the trees the color of hot cocoa with Hershey's syrup swirled in. Though every tree, every blade of grass, is the exact same color as the others, as if a little kid colored it all in with one box of markers. That's funny.

The smells are stronger here too—the forest pine smell is almost overwhelming, mixed with the wild scent of the lion. I gag a little at how strong it is.

My blood is still flying around my body too fast, and my head is pounding. I was happy in the air, and when we landed, but I didn't like the lion at all. I don't like lions even at the zoo. They pace back and forth, trapped, and stare at people like we'd make a good mouthful if they could only reach.

Now I'm standing in front of a group of kids who are staring at me like I'm the one in the cage . . . like at home. Groups of people are always scary, and other kids can be the worst. I look away and rub my hand hard against my lips, back and forth, back and forth. It helps distract from the scariness, to feel my fingers on my lips, familiar, soft.

When I look up, they're all rubbing their mouths too. They're making fun of me. My heart sinks in my chest.

But then Peter does it too, and not one of them is laughing.

I frown, trying to understand. Maybe they just think that's what we do when we meet people, and they're being polite. I look at Clover. She laughs and rubs her mouth too, and then I laugh and laugh, my belly full of laughing. A few of the kids laugh too. As soon as I stop rubbing, everyone else stops.

"I'm Fergus," I say, feeling suddenly bold.

"And I'm Clover," she says.

They make a circle around the three of us, Peter and Clover and me, and say their names. The pixies make big swoops in the air. The tall boy who spoke first is named Friendly, and there's a girl named Shoe and another girl named Rella, but I get caught up thinking about how your name could be Shoe, and I don't remember the rest. Hopefully, they'll say them again later. I should've recorded them, so I'd know.

"We saw the cat run away," Rella says. She's very small, with pale skin, freckles, and straight coppery hair. She shoves it out of her eyes. "Well done, Peter."

"Wasn't it?" Peter says. The bow and arrow are slung on his back now. "I knew I could make him run without a fight." The pixies dive at Peter, hovering in front of his face, and he laughs. "Yes, it was you, too." He turns to me. "What kind of beast was that?"

I'm pleased that he asked me and not Clover—everyone always asks Clover. I stammer a little, but I squeeze the words out. "M-m-mountain lion. Or cougar."

"Cou-gar," the girl called Shoe tries. "Cougar." She shuffles her feet like she's doing a dance, and I want to join in. I tap my feet a little. "It'll be fun to have new beasts and foes," she adds. Her skin is a rich red-brown, and she has black eyes with long eyelashes. Her hair is all the way down her back, curly and tangled. I think her color is blue, shifting blue like the ocean. When her eyes meet mine, I look down. I might have been staring.

"Foes?" Clover asks.

"Of course," Peter says. "There must always be foes for adventures. Different foes for everyone who visits. But it's been long and long since we had visitors." He's quiet for a bit, so I look at him. His face is scrunched up, but I don't know what that means. Then he bows and stretches out an arm. "First we must show you our home. Wendy taught me that." He turns to Clover. "Your house—Wendy's house—fell down, so we used the wood for a great bonfire. We could build another house if you like. Or you could sleep underground with the rest of us."

"Underground is fine," Clover snaps. "I'm not different from anyone else."

Peter nods. "Off you get, Lost Boys." Everyone scatters to different trees. I see that every tree is hollow, with a big hole in each one. The Lost Boys (and Girls) slip into the hollows.

I stand with Peter and Clover, shifting back and forth. My feet want to run, to disappear with the others, but I don't know where to go. I look up at the orange-blue sunrise sky, clouds floating wispily. There's a cloud that looks like a cougar. I wonder if that's coincidence or magic.

"Why do you call them all Lost Boys, if there are girls too?" I ask Peter.

He shrugs. "We took a vote when we started having girls too. We change terms every once in a while. We were all Lost Girls for a while, but we're Lost Boys for the moment. Fergus, you shall fit in the biggest tree, same as me." He studies Clover. "You, the second biggest. They all go to the same place, so it's just which one fits you best."

"Is it time for bed now?" Clover asks. She yawns so big I can see her teeth. "We've been up all night."

Peter laughs. "We don't have bedtime. When you're tired, you lie down and sleep, day or night. Unless we're fighting, and then no one sleeps." He shrugs. "Except when we have a mother here. Wendy made us go to bed early, I remember, no matter what." He tilts his head at Clover, and raises an eyebrow. "Will you make us go to bed early?"

Clover frowns. "No bedtime is fine with me."

I don't think she means it. She usually loves enforcing bedtime when Mom's not home. I can't imagine Clover not following rules. She'll probably have everybody in bed by nine tomorrow, and then start making rules about everything else.

I'm going to enjoy it until she does.

Peter goes to a tree entrance—the third tree from a big fire pit—and points down. "Fergus, this one. We have ladders now instead of chutes. I think it was Margaret who added those."

Margaret, our grandmother. I try to picture her as she is now, plump and gray-haired, slipping down inside a tree. I laugh. It's a good image.

I slide over and look down the hole. It's dark, and seems tight, but neither of those things bothers me. I find the ladder, made of sticks and twine, and start down.

I stop halfway because I like it in here. The tree smells cool and damp but alive, like an old forest. Here in the middle it's dark and small, and just me. No one can watch me or hear me. I grip the ladder sticks, breathe, and feel myself relax, feel the stress seep out into the earth.

It's good to know I can come here if I want to calm down.

When I get to the bottom, it's loud, with all the Lost Boys running around and shouting. It's one big room with nine beds all along the edges, a stove on one side with a chimney going up, and a table in the middle. I stand there for a minute, one hand on the ladder, and watch. I could go back up if I want to, I tell myself. If it's too much, I could stay in the tree for a while.

I kind of want to stay in the tree.

But watching them run also makes me feel like

running too, so I decide to join in, even though I don't know the game. I don't think it matters. Peter comes down behind me and joins in. We run, and shout, and tag each other sometimes, until we all get tired and drop to the ground.

Friendly gets everyone bowls of some kind of stew, and we sit in a loose circle on the floor around the table and eat. Clover sits next to me, too close. I wish she'd sit on the other side and let me be. She's hovering like I'm going to do something wrong.

I frown at her over my bowl. The texture is funny, with some strange chunks I don't like, but it's warm and I'm hungry, so I eat everything but the chunks. Those I push aside and leave in a little pile in the bowl. I don't look at Clover in case that's wrong. Some of the Lost Boys laugh and talk, while others just eat quietly. One of them, little with blond hair down to his shoulders, goes and sits by himself by the fire, puts his feet up, and closes his eyes instead of eating.

I like that it feels free to do whatever you want here. I like that no one treats me differently, staring at how I look or eat or talk. I've never felt so able to do what I feel like. If Clover weren't watching me I wouldn't feel different at all.

"Where are the pixies?" I ask.

"Oh, they don't like it down here," Peter says. "Ever since Tinker Bell . . ." He makes a face. "Pixies don't live long, you know. Since Tinker Bell left us, a long time ago now, the other pixies won't come underground. But they have their own home, not far. Pixie Hollow."

The stew makes me sleepy, and I start to blink hard, to stay awake.

"Peter," Clover says. "I think Fergus and I need to sleep."

There it is. I knew she'd start telling me what to do.

"Don't want to sleep," I snap. "You sleep."

She blinks at me, her mouth turned down. "Fine, *I* need sleep." She rolls her eyes. I hate it when she does that.

Peter points out two beds near each other, near the tree I came down. Clover stumbles to one and collapses, curling up under a blanket. I fold my arms. I don't want to go to bed just because she did. I can stay up at least five minutes longer. I count.

I make it two and a half—one hundred and fifty seconds—and then go lie down. I am tired. The bed is bumpy, though, and smells musty and strange, and I don't like it. My body tenses up, and for a while I feel like I might need to scream or run or go back in the tree.

But I don't want Clover to come help me. I don't

want to need help. I'm in a different place now, a new place. Everything's different.

I'm in a *story*.

I focus hard on my breath, on listening to the fire crackle and the Lost Boys chatter, and before I know it my body relaxes and I fall asleep. I don't know how it's peaceful, with no one even being quiet, but it is.

Clover

I wake to Peter standing over me. "Clover," he says, and I can tell it's not the first time he's said it. "We must go."

I sit up, rubbing at my cheeks. "What time is it?"

Peter shrugs. "There are no clocks in the Neverland anymore, not since the crocodile's tick stopped. But it's time to get out of bed. Our adventure has begun."

"Adventure?" I yawn. "Okay." I look over at the bed next to me, but it's empty. I get an instant burst of worry. "Where's Fergus?"

"He is already aboveground, making ready with the others." He smiles, his baby teeth showing. "He is easier to wake."

I snort. Not usually. Usually I'm the one up first, to the alarm, making sure we're fed and ready for school. Or Mom gets me up with a kiss, and then we have to drag Fergus out of bed.

Does Mom know we left? Is she panicking back at home? Did we ruin her peaceful studying time? I didn't think of that before. I just followed Fergus, and Peter, without considering Mom enough. How long will we even be here?

I stand, brush off my wrinkly clothes, and redo my bun. I decide not to brush my teeth, since they're waiting for me. I'll have to make sure I do it later.

"Fergus has eaten already, but we have food for you up there. Come up soon," Peter says from the bottom of the ladder. He tilts his head. "Wendy was always up first."

I groan. Of course she was.

"Wait," I say. "What's the adventure? Is it a good one?"

For a second his cheerful expression drops. "Not a good beginning, no. One of the mermaids has gone missing."

When I pop up only a few minutes later, my backpack on my shoulders and Fergus's in my hand, everyone else is standing in the middle of the clearing, ready to go . . . wherever we're going. The sun is directly above us, blindingly bright, so if it works the same as at home, I guess it's around noon. I was asleep for a long time. I hate sleeping in that late. I wonder what they were all doing while I was asleep.

I hope I don't have a mustache drawn on my face or anything.

"Fergus," I whisper, "here." I try to hand him his backpack, but he ignores me.

"Don't you want your backpack?"

He doesn't answer, just looks up at the sky, bouncing on his heels.

I set the backpack on the ground at his feet. He won't leave it there, not with his books in it.

Friendly hands me slices of some sort of sweet melon and smiles. "Happy thoughts," he says softly.

"Form up!" Peter calls. "To the lagoon, quickly!"

They get in a line so easily I can tell they must do it all the time. Peter, then Friendly, Shoe, Jumper, George, Rella, and Swim. Fergus goes next—his backpack on his back—then me at the end. I wish I knew what we're going to do when we get to the lagoon, but it *is* an adventure. I guess you don't plan an adventure.

I munch on the melon, which is delicious. It drips all over my hands, though, and there are no napkins. I wonder how Fergus dealt with that. He always likes to have his hands clean. I wipe mine on my jeans.

Two pixies come rocketing down from the sky and hover by Peter. From the way they're moving, I think they're talking to him. Maybe the pixies are upset about a missing mermaid too.

"It's like we're Odysseus," Fergus says over his shoulder. "*The Odyssey*. Odysseus."

"Doesn't that take ten years?" I ask.

Fergus nods happily, his hands flying. "*Odyssey*. Ten years to get back after the Trojan War. Odysseus kept getting lost, or the gods threw him off track." Peter whistles, and Fergus marches forward with the others. I look at the backs of the Lost Boys, then at the forest and the mountain rising above them. This place is pretty amazing. But I definitely don't want to be here for ten years.

"We follow the North Star!" Fergus hollers.

"Quiet march!" Peter calls back in a hoarse whisper. "We don't know what beasts are about today."

"We follow the North Star," Fergus whispers.

"We follow the North Star," Swim, a small, scraggly boy with blond hair, repeats with a smile.

I walk closer to Fergus and keep checking behind me, remembering the mountain lion. I wish I weren't last.

We follow a path that goes through trees for a while, then turns and goes uphill, toward the mountain. The trees are closer together here, and darker. Almost black. Lots of them are old and dead, their branches stretching across the path. A wind cuts through, colder than it should be on a tropical island. I shiver. "What is this place?" I whisper to the Lost Boys ahead of me.

Swim half turns and whispers back, "Shhh! This is the Haunted Forest. There are ghosts everywhere. The ghosts of pirates have been bad lately. George was grabbed right off the trail, and the rescue took us weeks."

George glances back at us, face serious, and I frown at Fergus. Ghosts of *pirates*? For real? "Be careful," I say.

Fergus frowns and keeps marching. I hunch my shoulders and follow. A cloud comes over the sun and it instantly gets twice as dark, twice as cold. I squeak, but no one hears me. I really don't like being at the back. The trail winds on, the trees reaching out for us with their bare branches like pointed fingers.

I see something move to the right, in the brush. Was that a mountain lion? A ghost? What do I do if a ghost grabs me? Will anyone even notice? I walk faster, almost at a trot, and bump into Fergus. He jumps away and keeps going.

There's a long, low howl close by. I freeze, but the

rest of them don't stop, so then I have to go faster again to keep up. We go up again, another steep hill. One at a time the others reach the top and disappear, until it's just me and Fergus I can see. Then Fergus crests the hill, and it's just me.

The howling comes again from behind me—"oooooooOOOOO." I run, my legs pumping.

At the top, everything changes in an instant. From here you can see it all, straight downhill to the ocean. The scary trees suddenly end, becoming tropical bushes and plants with huge leaves, and a few palm trees. The sun pops out too. The water dances in the distance, sunlight sparkling on every wave. It's all bright and clear and beautiful, a postcard picture of an island.

I look over my shoulder at the Haunted Forest, dark and menacing, lurking behind us. It would be easy to think I imagined it, imagined the fear, once I got up here. As soon as it was behind me.

Everyone else is already halfway down the hill, not looking back at all, so I follow, stepping carefully on the steep slope down. I still slide on the little rocks.

After the hill the path curves back and forth, like a snake, and then we come to a creek. It's too wide to jump over, fast and foamy. If I squint I can see the waterfall it comes from, far off to the left, bursting out of the mountain. Peter and the rest turn right and walk alongside the creek, toward the ocean. The creek dumps into one of the lagoons, far down. "Is that where we're going?" I ask.

This time Rella turns around. "That's Dragon Lagoon. We don't go there much during dragon season, unless we want a Real Adventure, or the dragon starts hunting pixies again and we have to stop her. We're going to Mermaid Lagoon."

"I liked it when we fought the dragon," Jumper says over her shoulder. "That was fun."

"Dragon Lagoon," Fergus says. "Dragon Lagoon."

"Too hard to say, right?" I reply. "It should be Dragon Lagon. Or Dragoon Lagoon."

Rella tilts her head but doesn't answer. She keeps walking.

"Dragon Lagon," Fergus says, and smiles.

"I like that one too." I smile back.

"Hush!" Peter calls. "Quiet march!"

We hush and keep going.

After a while we come to a partly flat log that hangs dangerously over the creek. A bridge, kind of. One by one Peter and the Lost Boys walk across, as easy as if it were nothing. No one looks back. Jumper hops across. Rella skips. I hang by the side, watching. I hate bridges.

Even driving over the Coronado Bridge at home with Mom makes me nervous. I have to sing under my breath the whole time to distract myself.

Fergus crosses fine and waits for me on the other side. So I have to go. I have to follow everyone else.

I set one foot on the log, then take it off. I can't. I might fall.

I look at Fergus. He doesn't say anything, just watches me, blinking. He knows it's hard for me. But then he looks over his shoulder at the rest of the Lost Boys already moving down the trail. He wants to go with them. We need to go. I need to be brave and do this.

Wendy would have done it, no problem. She'd already have been over the bridge. Mom probably would have too, if she had ever come here. She's brave. Grandmother probably ran across it.

I put my foot back on, and the log wobbles. I take a deep breath and put my other foot on, then take a step. It's okay. I can do it.

I try to run across, so I won't be as scared, like Grandmother would. Except I slip halfway, bang my leg on the log, and smash down, down, down into the icy water.

Fergus

I stand still for a second, not sure what to do. She fell into the creek. It's fast and full, and it's pulling her down already, tumbling her over. Do I jump in? Try to pull her out?

It's only for a second. Then I yell.

"Help!" I call as loud as I can. "Help us!" At the same time I run down the creek to try to catch Clover. I reach out as she tumbles past, but the water pulls her away and I miss. "Help!"

Then Peter is there, with the cluster of Lost Boys. The two pixies dive for the water, skimming above Clover. She spins around again onto her back, the backpack pulling her down, and screams.

"Friendly!" Peter commands. "Here!"

They run a few paces downstream and position themselves—Friendly's feet are in the creek—and each of them grabs one of Clover's arms as she goes by, neatly pulling her out of the water. I can tell they've done it before, probably lots. They pull her onto the grassy bank. She lies there with her arms stretched out, gasping and shivering. The water pours from her onto the ground.

I go and kneel next to her, the grass wet on my knees. "Are you all right?" I say, the words sticking in my throat. She doesn't answer, so I try again. "Are you okay?"

She nods, her eyes closed. Her hair is almost as dark as mine now, fallen out from her bun and dripping into the ground.

"Come now, Clover," Peter says, his fists on his hips. "That was a waste of time. I told you we had a mission. We do not have time to ride the stream down to the lagoon."

Clover props herself up on her elbows, blinking at him. The pixies buzz down close to her again, flying back and forth low over her.

"*And* it's dragon season," George adds with a glance at Peter. "We don't ride the stream in dragon season."

"Unless we want a Real Adventure," Jumper says, bouncing on her heels.

Clover frowns, and I recognize her danger face. I stand up.

"You think I did this on purpose?" she says, her voice hard.

"Now is not the time for riding," Peter says. "The mermaids—"

Clover sits up, nearly hitting one of the pixies. "I fell! I didn't jump in the icy creek to ride down to a lagoon where there's a dragon! Why would I do that?"

"Dragon," I whisper. "Dragon Lagon." I don't like the tension here, the anger I can feel. I take a step back, tapping my fingers.

Now Peter frowns. "You fell? Crossing the log bridge? No one has ever fallen off the log bridge."

The pixies move up the back of Clover's head, then down over her soggy backpack, and I suddenly see what they're doing. They're drying her. I don't think she knows it, though.

"Yes, I fell!" she says, loud. When she uses that voice, I go in the other room if I can. "I slipped! It was an accident!"

The Lost Boys murmur to each other, little puffs of conversation. Peter frowns at Clover, and Clover frowns at Peter. Her hair is almost dry now, and the pixies go to work on her clothes.

"It's all right," Shoe says, stepping between them. "Everything is all right now."

"Very well," Peter says at last. He sighs. "Let's keep going. Serena's message was urgent." Shoe puts out a hand and helps pull Clover up. Peter marches back up the hill, and the others fall into line behind him, including Shoe. Clover touches her clothes—almost dry—and then her hair. She looks wonderingly at the pixies as they fly back to Peter.

"They dried you," I say in a whisper. "Magic."

She nods and gets in line behind the smallest Lost Boy. I follow her this time, to make sure she's safe.

"Magic," I say again. "Real magic, like a story. We're in a story."

She looks back at me. "Magic, and pixies, and dragons." She shakes her head. "I still have a hard time believing any of it is real." She shrugs. "Is it real?"

"Real magic." I look around at the too-bright colors, the mountain poking up into the blue sky, the line of kids following Peter—who I still think might be Pan. "Do you think there will be stories about us someday? Like the stories of Wendy and John and Michael?"

Clover shrugs. "Maybe. Not good stories about me, though. I can't do anything right here."

We hurry to catch up with the others.

After a long time of walking, mostly on a dirt path through trees and big plants, we start down a hill to the other lagoon. Mermaid Lagoon. It really is just as blue as it looked from the air, a shimmering turquoise blue I don't have words for, shaped in almost a perfect circle with palm trees all around it. It smells interesting, too, like seaweed and fish and salt—like the beach at home, but stronger, richer. It's a pleasant smell. The sun sparkling on the water is bright, though. I shade my eyes to look out.

I don't see any mermaids yet, just the waves, and a big, flat rock a ways out in the middle of the lagoon. I love looking at the ocean. At home sometimes we take the bus to La Jolla and I sit on the grass on the cliffs, watching the waves roll in and out. It's the same rhythm, over and over. It's like the ocean is always rocking, soothing itself. Soothing me.

The rhythm here is the same as at home. I relax, watching it, and sway a little.

Then everyone marches down to the sand and gathers behind Peter, so I follow. The pixies stay back, up by the trees.

"Where are the mermaids?" I ask.

One of the girls—Rella—shushes me. "Peter has to call them. They're hiding until they know it's him."

Peter steps forward, his bare toes in the water, and whistles, a strange, high sound that makes me cover my ears. It doesn't last long, though.

Nothing happens for a few minutes, and I want to do something, move or ask another question, but I make myself wait. Finally a head comes out of the water, then another, and another, and I gasp.

There are eleven mermaids in the water, staring at us like we're the strange ones. And they are *beautiful*.

I don't normally pay much attention to girls, except Clover. They're awkward and they laugh more than boys do, which makes me uncomfortable. I always suspect they're laughing at me. But there's something about the mermaids I can't stop looking at.

"Wait till you hear them sing," Friendly says, next to me. "There's a reason mermaids can lure sailors."

I look hard at the sand, at the ripple marks the waves leave. I don't want to be *lured*.

"Peter," one of them says. "We live in hopes that you can help us."

"That's Serena," Friendly says. "She's the leader."

Her voice is beautiful too, the ringing of a bell. So beautiful it makes my chest ache.

"Mermaids are nymphs of the sea," I say to myself, very soft. "Called Nereids from their father Nereus. Thetis was a Nereid. Though in *Clash of the Titans* she's not a mermaid at all."

"Nymphs of the sea?" Friendly repeats. "I didn't know that."

"My sister Allora has been taken," the mermaid says. "Last night she was singing on the rock, after the rest of us had gone to the depths. Suddenly she stopped, mid-word—Allora would never do that—and when she did not begin again, I swam up to see why she had stopped. She was gone." Her voice changes, buckles, and I look at her. Tears are streaming down her face, dripping into the waves. Some of the other mermaids start crying too, with quiet gasps.

It makes me hurt inside. I wish I could comfort them, but I wouldn't begin to know how. I kick my feet in the sand. George takes a step forward. Then another. Rella does too.

Peter paces back and forth along the water. "Were there any clues? Any other sounds or traces?"

"I thought I heard barking, and growling," one of the other mermaids says, so low I have to strain to hear her. I take a step closer, the waves almost touching my shoes. George and Rella are in the water now, up to their ankles. "I do not know this sound for certain. Dogs, perhaps? Or wolves?"

All the mermaids murmur that yes, they heard barking too. One of them looks directly at me, her eyes a dark, dark brown, almost black. I breathe through my nose. I can't look away, can't look at the sand. I want to dive right in, to follow her. I take another step. The water sloshes in my shoes, but I don't even care.

"Very well," Peter says. "This is our adventure. We will find and rescue Allora." He looks at the Lost Boys—George and Rella up to their knees, me and Swim with our feet wet—then back to the mermaids. "Enough temptation. We'll be dragging them out of the water soon. You should go."

The first mermaid nods, and they all, as one, disappear beneath the waves.

I desperately wish I could jump in after them.

Clover

The Lost Boys all stand staring at the water, half of them standing in it. Except for Shoe and Peter, they all seem a bit fuzzy and confused. Even Fergus. "What was *that*?" I ask.

Peter shoves a hand through his hair. "*That* is why I'm usually the only one who talks to the mermaids. They're irresistible to some." He shrugs at me and Shoe. "To most. And they weren't even trying to do it. When they sing . . ." He shrugs again. "Even I want to go sometimes."

"Mermaids are Nereids," Fergus says in a flat voice. He's staring at the sand. "Or Oceanids, or nymphs.

Depending on the source. Thetis was a Nereid. Thetis was a Nereid."

"You're okay now," I say. "They're gone."

He rubs his mouth hard, and when he glances up at me his eyes clear, and he seems normal. All of them seem to come out of it, talking again, though no one mentions what happened. How they all were staring at the ocean, fascinated, like they wanted to jump in and drown.

"Peter has strict rules about not coming here alone," Shoe says to me in a whisper. Her skin almost glows in the sun, a warm, orangish bronze. She's tall, several inches taller than me. She tugs on her long black hair, which is tied roughly into a knot but spraying out in wild strands all around her face.

I think suddenly that her hair should be braided, so it'd stay out of her way—like Mom taught me to do.

My stomach hurts and I press it, hard. I miss Mom so much I want to curl up and cry. I want to be *home*, with her. I'm not sure how we ended up here.

"Everyone to me!" Peter calls. "We need a plan of attack."

We sit in a circle on the beach, with Peter standing in the middle. I sit between Fergus and Shoe. Fergus scoops up a handful of sand and lets it trickle through his fingers, the light sparkling in it. He holds it up high, and it rains in front of his face. Some of the Lost Boys start punching each other and laughing, but Peter shushes them. The pixies come closer again, circling around Peter.

"We must cogitate," he says. He looks at each of us, his face serious. "This is not as straightforward as many of our adventures. First we must find what happened to Allora before we can defeat our foe."

"If there is a foe," I say.

Peter turns a glare on me, and I shrink back. In the book he's unpredictable, kind of a tyrant. But then he laughs.

"If? There is always a foe. That is why it is an *adventure*." He stomps one foot on the ground. "But why would a foe steal a mermaid? This has not happened before . . . except when the pirates were here. They tried. But they never got far. The mermaids have always been too powerful for any human."

"Maybe it's not a human," Rella says. "What barks? Dogs, and wolves. But do those live in the water? Are there sea dogs?"

"Sea lions," I say. "In San Diego there are sea lions, and they sound like they're barking. I've heard of them attacking people who threaten them, but mostly they're peaceful."

Peter tilts his head. "Sea lions," he says, like he's

feeling the words. "We will consider those as a possibility. What else? Fergus?"

Fergus folds his hands together and brings them close to his face. "There is Cerberus," he answers. "That is the three-headed, serpent-tailed dog that guards the underworld. And Fenris, the wolf who will kill Odin at Ragnarok." He frowns. "Those wouldn't be near the ocean. Sometimes the Vikings were called sea wolves, but that was only a name." He taps his fingers on his cheeks. "I think there was a sea dog in Irish mythology. . . ." He stills, and frowns again. "Yes. The Dobhar-chú. Sea hound. But that has only ever been seen in Ireland."

When he stops, there's silence. I'm afraid they're going to say something mean, make fun of him like the kids at home do, for knowing so much. It's just because he reads so much, because he's interested.

"Wow," Friendly says. "You know so many stories. Will you tell us stories tonight?"

The rest of them shout agreement, asking for stories.

Fergus smiles, but doesn't answer.

"Are there any other beasts from your home that could steal a mermaid?" Peter asks. "Or are there other stories you know from your land?"

It's like being in school. I desperately want to be the one with the answer. "Werewolves?" I say. "They're not from our land, but they're humans who become wolves on the full moon?"

"Do they swim in the ocean?" Peter asks.

I shake my head. I guess that wasn't the best idea. I dig my hands in the sand, like Fergus. It's dry, and falls right through my fingers. One of the pixies zips by in front of me, pauses for a second, and then moves on.

"Perhaps we need to find Allora first," Peter says. "Then we can face the foe. He will probably reveal himself when we locate her." He drops to the sand suddenly, sitting cross-legged. His back is to me.

It doesn't mean anything, I think. His back has to be to someone—it's a circle. It probably doesn't mean anything.

"We should climb the mountain!" Jumper says. "We can see if we can spot the mermaid or any dog creatures from there. Sea lions or"—she waves at Fergus—"what he said. Or any other clues."

"Or we could stay here and watch," Swim adds, a hopeful look on his face. "In case the mermaids are still in danger and it tries again."

It's quiet for a few seconds. Then Peter jumps to his feet, dives outside the circle, and runs around it, full speed. All the Lost Boys hold up their arms, and he slaps their hands as he goes by, like a strange game of Duck,

Duck, Goose. After he goes around once, he jumps into the middle again and collapses, lying on his back in the sand.

Why did he do that?

Fergus laughs, and so does everyone else. I don't understand. I grab another handful of sand, watch the tiny grains flow through my hands. The ocean beats against the shore a few steps away, the sun high overhead. One of the mermaids pokes her head above the water, looks at us, then goes below again. I think I'm the only one who saw her.

"Clover and Shoe," Peter says, startling me. It *is* like class, and I was just called on. "You two stay here and watch the beach. You seem to be immune to the call of the mermaids. The rest of us . . ." He waves his arms for them to get up, and everyone, including Fergus, pops to their feet. "Let's go climb the mountain!"

Panic floods me. "I should go with Fergus."

Peter frowns. "Why?"

Fergus looks at me. All of them do, all those eyes. I don't know how to explain. Because he's *autistic,* I want to say. Because he doesn't like to go on new adventures by himself. Because he might get upset, or lose his speech for a while, or have a meltdown. Because he might need me to help him. Because it's my job to help him. I promised Mom.

"You stay. I want to go," Fergus says. He stares at his feet, his hands curled in fists. I can see he wants this. Back home, he never really would've wanted to go.

Back home, he wouldn't have been asked.

I get it, suddenly. Here they don't see him that way. They don't know anything about autism, or what's "normal" and what isn't. Here he's just Fergus to them, like he is for me.

I nod, and they all cheer—Friendly and Jumper and George and Rella and Swim—and take off running toward the mountain. I watch them go, skipping and laughing. I don't like it. I don't like letting him out of my sight, especially in a place with random lions and dangerous streams and pirate ghosts and who knows what else. But I guess I have to.

One of the mermaids comes up out of the water again, then another, and another. Two of them climb onto the rock and lie there in the sun, basking like they're on beach chairs. Like sea lions. The others whisper to each other. I can tell they're still upset by their friend's disappearance. And scared, probably.

They look different from the mermaids in Disney movies. They're not all wearing shiny cloth bikini tops, for one thing. They have different style tops, most made out of seaweed. A few of the styles are from different plants. A couple of the mermaids don't have tops at all.

The mermaids *are* all strangely beautiful—but they're not all the same, like models or dolls. They're all different body sizes and shapes, with different faces and different skin colors, just like people back home. One of the mermaids on the rock has pale pink skin, and one has dark skin, her hair spiraling down her back in neat twists. I sit and watch them talking together, the sun shining on the waves. I don't want to follow them into the water—but it does look nice.

Shoe smiles at me, her arms circled around her legs, and I smile back. I can still hear the rest of the Lost Boys going up the path, their laughter echoing back to us. I wish I were going too. At the same time, it's nice to have a moment of quiet, just us and the mermaids. I look again at the one with the twists.

"Shoe," I say, "want me to braid your hair?"

She shrugs. "I don't know what that means. But yes!"

Fergus

They wanted me to come.

I hug the thought to myself as I run up the path, solidly in the middle of the group. I wasn't picked last, like in gym. They didn't groan when they "had to" take me. They cheered. And I'm not even last in line. I'm not a fast runner—I trip sometimes when everything feels uneven—but I'm keeping up. Clover, who's always solid and in charge and first, was the one who fell into the creek. She's the one who was left behind.

My hands fly up as I run. I feel the air under and around my palms, smell the sea, and laugh.

I like this place.

Rella, behind me, laughs too and waves her hands like mine. Friendly, just ahead, reaches down into the creek and flicks water at us, with a whoop, and then I do it back, the water cold on my hands. It feels good and I stop, dipping both hands in the water. I swirl them back and forth, watching the water ripple, following my movement. Swim dips his hands in too, beside me. One of the pixies skims along the surface of the water, a beautiful glowing ball.

"Lost Boys!" Peter calls sternly from the front. "Move on!"

I frown. Before we came here, I didn't picture Peter being strict or telling us what to do. But I guess he is the leader. We keep jogging forward.

It gets steeper, more mountain than hill now. It also gets louder. The waterfall is not far above us, the water pounding on the rock, foaming and churning at the bottom in a small pool. Every step we take, it gets louder, more insistent. The path winds right by it, the spray soaking the dirt, and then curves by, on up the mountain.

The sound bothers me. It feels like pressure pushing in at my ears, so steady and loud. I wish it would stop just for a few seconds. I clench my fists. I know we have to keep going, move past it, and then it will be better.

But it'll take so long. I don't know if I can stand it for that long.

We keep hiking, slower now. It's hard to run on this steep, narrow path, and the cliff drops off to our right, the creek rushing by below. A few drops of water spatter the path. We're getting close to the waterfall now.

It's so loud. I hate it. I cover my ears, but that only blocks the roar a little bit. The pressure builds, pushing at my ears, and I feel like I might need to scream. And then what will I do? Just scream, here, with everyone? With no Clover? I mimic the sound of the water, the *whoosh,* but it doesn't help.

I hear something else through my hands, something that's not the waterfall pounding. Rhythm. Voices.

I lift my hands. All the Lost Boys are singing. Or chanting, a marching song.

> *Left, right, left*
> *We're off on an adventure*
> *Left, right, left*
> *We're going to fight a foe!*
> *Left, right, left*
> *No beast will ever stop us*
> *Left, right, left*
> *The Lost Boys we will go!*

They start again, the same words, and I find myself singing along, chanting and marching in time. We pass right by the waterfall, the water splashing our feet, and then go on, away and up, the roar lessening. We keep singing, cheering, and I don't need to scream anymore.

I really like this place a lot.

I wonder what Mom would think of me being in Neverland.

Why did Mom choose not to come to Neverland? Why didn't she ever tell us about it?

I used to imagine, because I never knew our dad, that I was really the son of a god, like Percy Jackson. Maybe the son of Hermes. But I never thought we'd be related to the kids from Peter Pan, for real.

Maybe it's both. Maybe Peter is Hermes's son, and so am I, so we're really half brothers. . . .

"Fergus!" Peter calls, sharp. "Watch your feet!"

I jerk, and look where I am. I'm standing right at the edge of the path. We've reached the top of the mountain. There's nothing in front of me but air and a glorious view: the slope down, the bright crayon trees, the dry brown of the Haunted Forest, the brilliant lagoons. I think I can even see a big bulk of purple in Dragon

Lagoon. (Dragon Lagon!) After that, in all directions, all I see is the wide sweep of ocean, with clouds stretching thin overhead. There's no other land anywhere in sight—not even any rocks. I almost can't breathe at the beauty of it.

I step back so my feet are more safely on the path. I wonder what we're supposed to be looking for up here.

Peter eyes the pixies dancing near his head. "You don't see anything either?" He plucks a giant leaf from a nearby plant, rolls it into a telescope-like tube, and scans below, especially around Mermaid Lagoon. "It must be underwater, then. There is nothing else. But dogs, underwater?"

I can see the mermaids from here, if I squint. They're out again, tails breaching as they swim. I think I see the shapes of Clover and Shoe on the beach.

"We need more clues," Peter says. Then he shrugs. "But they will be revealed. Neverland always gives us enough to solve the mystery, when we need it. Now is not the time. While we wait, and think . . ." He grins, his teeth flashing white. "I call a Feast tonight."

All the Lost Boys cheer, so I cheer too. A feast. A large, abundant meal in celebration. There was a feast in the Underworld, called the Feast of Goibhniu, where Goibhniu gave his guests food that made them immortal.

On one side a feast might be loud and bright and wild, and that part makes me a little nervous. It might be overwhelming. On the other side it might be fun. The Lost Boys have been fun, so far. I bet I can spin and spin on the sand, and no one will mind. Maybe I can even go into the ocean. I hardly ever get to do that.

They dance, each one flailing in their own way, leaning their heads back and yelling, "Feast!"

I dance too, waving my hands, wiggling my arms, and lift my face to the sun. "Feast!" I call, as loud as I can, the sound filling my body, the dancing filling my whole self with sunshine, with release.

I feel so free, in a way I don't think I've ever felt before.

I wonder if Neverland is where I was really meant to be all along.

Clover

I sit behind Shoe on the beach, her hair twisted in my hands. It's so long, to the middle of her back, and thick, a shiny, deep black. I had to finger comb it for a long time just to get most of the knots out, but it's smoother now, enough to wrangle into a French braid. I even have a piece of seaweed next to me to tie it off when I'm done. Shoe seems happy, making little crooning noises to herself. What would it be like to never have had your hair braided? To have been here for years, or always? To never have a family other than the Lost Boys?

I can't imagine it. No school, no Mom. No adults.

No rules except what Peter says. Fergus seems to like it. But I couldn't stay here that long. I'd miss everything at home. I'd miss *real life*.

I'd miss Mom.

The mermaids are mostly in clusters, still talking, a few playing catch with bubbles. Keeping on with every-day things, in spite of being worried. I know what that feels like. I do it all the time, in small ways. Upset about that unfair grade in English? Shove it down. Mad at a friend who talked about me behind my back? Forget it. Tired from a long day of school and homework and helping Mom? Keep going. There's always the next thing to plan, to worry about.

Sometimes I wish I could let go and cry, or scream, or just yell *no!* But I can't. I have to be calm and in con-trol. That's what Mom expects.

Even here they want me to be the mother.

I tie off Shoe's braid and admire it. I wish I could show it to her, but without a phone to take a picture—or even a mirror—she'll have to trust me.

"It looks good," I say.

She smiles, pats her hair, and then stands and does a cartwheel. Then another one. She spins around, stretch-ing her arms wide. "It stays! Even when I flip! How did you do that?"

I bite my lip. "My mom taught me."

She does another flip. "I remember my mother a little," she says. "She had soft hands. I remember . . ." She scrunches her nose. "A pattern on her hands? There was a swirl, and a flower, winding down her wrist in brown . . ." She sighs. "It isn't much."

I lean back on the sand. "How did you get the name Shoe?"

She frowns, her eyebrows pulled together.

"You don't have to answer if you don't want to," I say.

She sits next to me and traces a circle in the sand. Then she sighs and wipes it out. "I got the name because of a shoe I brought with me." Her voice is quiet. "I was really little when I came here, and I didn't have anything of my own—except a shoe I was holding in my arms. I wouldn't let go, not for days. Wouldn't talk to anyone, even Peter."

She goes still, staring out at the water. I have no idea what to do, or say. One of the mermaids does a leap and dives back down, like a dolphin.

"What kind of shoe was it?" I ask after a while.

She swallows, hard. "A shoe with a tall heel. Silver, with sparkles all over it. My mother's . . . ?" Her voice cracks. "It must have been my mother's. I still have it, under my bed. It almost fits me now."

"I'm sorry," I whisper. "Do you ever . . . want to go back? Try to find her?"

She shakes her head, her eyes dark. "Peter says we only come here if we have no place else to go. That we're supposed to forget about all that and just live in the moment."

I wonder if that's true. We're quiet again for a while. The waves go in and out, in and out, like breathing.

Shoe takes a deep breath. "Why is your name Clover?"

I shrug. "My father named me. And it made my mom laugh, so she kept it. But then he died, after Fergus was born."

We stare out at the ocean for another long moment; then Shoe squeezes my hand. "This is far too sad. No sadness allowed on Neverland! We need our own adventure, to shake us out of this."

I frown. "But we're supposed to stay on the beach."

She shrugs. "Rules are made to be broken here. And I have a wonderful idea. Do you wish to go see Pixie Hollow?"

I want to say no right away—we're supposed to stay on the beach. That's what Peter said. But I'm in Neverland, not school. "Where's Pixie Hollow?"

Shoe springs up. "It's the most beautiful place, hidden in the forest. Not far." She tugs on her braid and grins. "The pixies probably won't be there now, because they'll all be following Peter. So we can take a peek. Shall we?" She holds out her hand.

I look at the mermaids. I *should* stay here and make sure they're okay. Then I look at Shoe, her eyes bright, her smile wide and open. I want to be like that. Fun, not worried all the time.

I take her hand and let her tug me up.

"Let's go to Pixie Hollow!" I say.

Shoe laughs. She runs into the surf and says something to Serena, the leader of the mermaids. As soon as Shoe's on dry sand again, she bursts into a run, toward the side of the island we haven't been to before. "Race you!" she yells over her shoulder.

I take off, my heart lifting. The sun is warm on my head, the sand flying up under my feet, a friend with me. This is an adventure. *Our* adventure.

After we leave the beach we slow down and walk on the path, side by side. We push our way up into the brush, past what looks like an old orchard. The trees are all in neat rows, but clearly nobody takes care of them anymore. There are weeds and flowers everywhere, and the trees are old and gnarled, but heavy with small red apples. I think how much Fergus would want to explore in there.

I hope he's doing okay. I feel a pang of guilt. I should've been worrying about that before.

No. He's adventuring, and I am too.

The path curves back to the ocean, on a cliff that overlooks a weirdly shaped rock that Shoe calls Skull Rock—she makes a creepy face, which makes me laugh—and then back inland, toward the mountain. Just when I start to think it's been a long time, Shoe stops at the top of a rise and points down into what looks like a miniature forest. Everything is smaller, even the trees. I can just see tiny little houses nestled in them. "That is Pixie Hollow."

It looks peaceful, private. "Are you sure it's okay if we go down there?"

Shoe raises her eyebrows and gives me a mischievous smile. "Truth? It's not exactly *encouraged*. But we'll be fine, right? What's an adventure if it's something you're supposed to do?"

I hesitate. But she's right. Neverland. No rules. Embrace it.

"This time I'm going to win," I say, and race down the hill, straight into Pixie Hollow.

Shoe wins, but I slide in just behind her, panting, and look around in amazement. The trees come up to my waist, the bushes and flowers only to my ankles. I can stand here and see over the treetops of this whole little valley. The path narrows too, one foot taking up the whole width of it. Shoe and I can't even stand side by side.

"I feel like a giant," I whisper, and even that sounds loud, booming across the trees.

"We *are* giants in this place," Shoe whispers back. "But come down here. You need to see."

She crouches down on her heels, so I do too. I gasp. It's so beautiful. The tiny trees are in bloom, with so many shades of color I couldn't even name them all. There's a little pond set back in the hollow, the sun sparkling on the clear, rippling water. There's an active orchard, with apples, pears, and oranges the size of walnuts. But the most amazing part is the houses. Miniature houses hang from trees, or are tucked on the ground, with neat rows of tiny flowers in front of them. Each house is different, with its own style. There are windows as big as my thumb, with real glass. Bright red and blue doors, with shiny door knockers. Front paths with miniature shells laid as paving stones. I fall to my knees, staring.

"It's a real fairyland," I say.

"Isn't it?" Shoe answers. "I only came here once, when I was small, and I didn't stay long. But I remember it always, like a dream."

"Why didn't you come back?" I ask.

She frowns. "Peter told me not to. He is very strict about it. I always meant to anyway, though."

I don't like that at all. Why is Peter strict about it?

But I can't stop staring. I've always liked miniature things, dollhouses and models. I used to spend hours at the railroad museum in San Diego, studying all the mini scenes while Fergus watched the trains. But this is real. And there are so many houses. There must be more pixies than I thought.

"But where are all the pixies?" I ask. "They can't all be with Peter."

Suddenly I'm slammed onto my back, with dozens of balls of light crashing into me together. They sting—tiny fierce pinches all over my arms, my legs, my belly, my face. I close my eyes against the blinding light and try to scream, but something stings my tongue, and I shut my mouth again. I try to swat them away, but my arms are pinned down, balls of light on top of them. I can't move my legs, either. The stings don't stop. Panic overwhelms me. This is probably poison. I can't escape. I'm going to die here, on my back in the middle of Pixie Hollow.

Because I broke the rules *once*.

Fergus

We're dancing on the top of the cliff, our arms raised high, when two balls of light—pixies—come flying in fast, diving to Peter. He goes still, listening, and his face gets serious.

"Lost Boys!" he says. "Someone is invading Pixie Hollow! Let us go and fight them! Grab weapons as you go. Save the pixies!"

Everyone moves together into a line, like it's a dance they know, and Peter starts marching down the path.

I stand there, not sure what to do. I don't know how to fight. I don't know what to grab as a "weapon" or how I'd use it. Do they have battle formations they use?

I've studied some of the Greek battle formations, but I don't *know* them. Would I only get in the way?

It's the first time I've felt out of place since we've been here.

Rella notices me and winks. "Don't worry—we'll win," she says. "We always win. Come on!" She breaks out of line to pull me into it, behind her, and then it's our turn to march. Jumper starts to sing, and all the others join in, so I do too. I know the words now.

> *Left, right, left*
> *We're off on an adventure*
> *Left, right, left*
> *We're going to fight a foe!*

We go down the mountain another way, toward a rock that's shaped like a skull. Sometimes Lost Boys break off and dive into the trees, coming back with sticks, or big rocks. Peter picks up a bow and arrow he must have hidden in a tree. At some point, Swim taps me on the back and hands me a long, heavy stick. I might have used it for a walking stick at home. It's rough against my palms.

"Shhh!" Peter loud-whispers. He raises a hand. "I think I hear something."

We all stop, and I look around. I wasn't really paying attention to where we were going. We're in another forest, with more of the bright green trees. A stream trickles nearby. There are leaves under our feet, muffling our sound. The pixies fly ahead, then come back fast and buzz around Peter. He makes a signal and moves forward down the hill, all the Lost Boys crowding behind him.

"Intruders!" he shouts. "Stay where you are, or we will have to attack you!"

I grip the stick tight in my hand and peer over Rella's shoulder to see.

It's Clover and Shoe, lying on the ground. And a whole lot of angry pixies swarming over them.

"No!" I say, my voice high. "That's Clover!"

"And Shoe!" Friendly says.

There's a pause, then Peter says something, and the pixies all move away at once. Clover and Shoe stand up shakily. Clover seems okay, except for the red dots all over her skin. Both of them have them. Shoe's hair is in a half braid, hair hanging out on the side like a flag.

Peter stamps down the hill, his bow still out. His ears are bright pink. "Clover. Shoe. You should not have come here. This is a private place. Pixies already have to deal with a world that is not their size—they need their own place to come back to, free from humans and mermaids and beasts. They don't need us spying on them."

The pixies do look angry, like wasps when you take down their nest. They float in an angry barricade in front of a cluster of tiny houses.

Clover hangs her head, and Shoe kicks at the dirt.

"Apologize to them!" Peter points to the pixies. "Now!"

Clover gulps so loud I can hear it from up here. "I'm sorry. I didn't mean to upset you." Her voice is quavery. "I didn't know."

"Didn't you?" Peter says in a voice that sounds like Mom's. "Shoe? I know you knew better."

Shoe looks at her feet. "Sorry."

Peter nods and turns to the wall of pixies. He bows. "We apologize for the intrusion. It will not happen again. We are having a Feast tonight at Mermaid Lagoon. Of course you are invited." He glances over his shoulder. "Clover and Shoe, you will not have sweets."

I guess there are rules and punishments in Neverland after all. Clover looks like she wants to disappear.

"A Feast?" Shoe says hopefully.

Peter smiles, and it's like none of that ever happened. "A Feast!" he replies. "We must prepare. Lost Boys, to the beach!"

Some of the food for the Feast is invisible.

No one else mentions this, or even seems to think it's strange. There are platters of fruit—mangoes, which I won't even touch because they're slimy, and pineapple, oranges, and bananas. There's a big platter of fish that the mermaids contributed, roasted over the fire, and a plate of bite-size honey cakes the pixies brought. Clover asks Shoe why the mermaids would eat fish, when they're "part fish," but Shoe explains that they're not fish at all. They're a separate species.

I knew that already. They're Nereids. Clover should have asked me.

There's a bowl of boiled eggs, tiny eggs with shells that are slightly blue or slightly brown.

Everything is served on hollowed-out slabs of wood. The jugs of juice are made out of hardened mud or clay, except for one glass one, filled with a pink liquid.

Then there are three platters, mixed in with the others, that are just empty.

We line up, smaller wood slabs in our hands, to take some food, and I stop at the first empty one.

"Make sure to try the beast!" Jumper says. She pretends to take some with her hands, like she's doing

improvisation. We do that at the Autism Center sometimes. They say it helps to visualize things before you see
them for real.

I frown and look at Clover behind me. She shrugs.
"There's invisible food in the book, too," she whispers.
"Just pretend."

I don't want to. It seems wrong, silly. But I reach out
and act like I'm picking some meat up with my hand.
A drumstick, maybe. I like drumsticks, as long as they
don't have any sauce on them. The weird thing is, it almost feels like I do have something in my hand. Clover
pretends to take some too.

I take a real banana, and an orange, and skip the fish.
It smells fishy. I take honey cakes. I stop at the next
empty platter.

"What's that?" I ask George.

George looks surprised. "You don't see it? That's
your favorite meal. I have enchiladas. I remember those
from when I was small. Shoe has hoppers. No one knows
what Peter has, but he always gobbles it up."

I stare at the plate. It's different for everyone? How
could that be? How would that work? Magic, I guess.
Or just imagination, if there isn't really anything there.

What would I have if I could have anything? That's
easy. Grilled cheese.

I pretend to take a grilled cheese sandwich, and I al-most smell the cheese, the buttery bread. This one is the kind of cheese I like, plain American. My mouth waters.

"It's your favorite meal," I tell Clover. "Favorite ever."

She scrunches her face, scratching at her bumpy arm. "I can't even think of what I want. Anything?"

"Favorite ever," I say.

"Pasta carbonara," she says. "Like Mom makes. With peas." She reaches out and scoops with her hand, but then her face changes. She drops the invisible pasta onto her plate and wipes her hand on her jeans.

"I felt it," she whispers. "For a second it was there."

"It's magic," I say. "Because we're in a story."

"The sweets plate is last," George says. "That's even better."

"Do you think they have chocolate chip cookies on the sweets plate?" I ask Clover.

She shrugs, her face tight. "I bet they do."

I forgot: she can't have any.

I pretend to pick up a chocolate chip cookie and then go sit on the sand by Friendly and Shoe. We're way high up on the beach, and the mermaids are far out by the rock, with food spread out on it. I think Peter took it to them.

I can hear them splashing out there. I feel the pull tugging at my chest a little bit. I watch the waves instead. In and out, in and out. I think the ocean is the best place ever.

The pixies are here too, all of them buzzing around in their own area a little ways off. I wonder if they're still mad at Clover. She doesn't look at them.

The sun starts to drop, pink spreading across the sky like Apollo is dragging it behind his cart. I nod to Apollo and eat. The honey cakes are delicious, and the banana and orange are sweet and just the right amount of ripe. I wish I could eat the invisible grilled cheese, but I can't remember where it was on the plate, so I can't find it again. I pretend to eat the beast meat, even though I don't know what kind of beast it's supposed to be. I think I taste it a little. Like chicken.

The cookie I completely taste, warm with the chocolate perfectly melty.

I like eating here. At home there's a lot of pressure about eating—you have to do it at a certain time, the same time as everyone else, whether you're hungry or not. You're supposed to eat the same food everyone else is eating, even if you don't like it. It doesn't make sense. I don't like most of the foods other people like. Here nobody seems to worry about it.

"Finish your fruit," Clover says, and I grind my teeth. *She* seems to worry about it. But no one else.

When we're done eating, Friendly and Jumper start a bonfire with some sticks and logs from a pile under the trees. I make my hands fly, and hop on the sand. Mom and Clover and I have been to beach bonfires a couple times, and I like them. The smoke smells like summer, and the crackling is soothing. It doesn't have a pattern, but it has a rhythm. You can see it in the flames, too: a dance. I squat down by it, dig my toes in the sand, and watch the orange flame catch, spreading from wood to wood.

"Clover, will you sing?" Peter asks. "The song you sang to Fergus when I listened at the window."

Everyone goes quiet. I glance at Clover. She has her scared look, but then she swallows, and nods. I clap my hands. I always like to listen to Clover sing.

Clover

Singing. I can do that, even if I can't adventure properly. I know how to sing. I take a sip of water, then a deep breath.

"*Alouette, gentille alouette.*"

The quiet in the circle gets deep. Even the mermaids stop splashing to listen.

"*Alouette, je te plumerai. Alouette, gentille alouette. Alouette, je te plumerai.*"

I sing and sing, my eyes closed. It feels like my voice is the only sound other than the waves and the fire. It's almost the feeling I had with my happy thought. With everyone listening to me, I feel strong, powerful. Peaceful.

When I finish, there's a long pause before anyone moves again.

"That was amazing!" Shoe says softly. "You should sing something else." The others murmur agreement, and George even claps.

I feel like maybe I could fly right now even without pixie dust.

Before I can reply, one of the mermaids starts singing, out on the flat rock. The one with the twisted hair. Her voice is soprano, eerie and beautiful.

"She's competing with you," Shoe says, laughing. "Jasmina is a little competitive about singing."

I almost recognize the song. Not the words—it's a language I've never heard—but the melody is familiar. We all sit perfectly still, listening, like we're in a trance.

Suddenly I hear something else, faint, messing with the perfection of the song. What is that?

Jasmina keeps singing, sitting up high on the rock. She lifts her chin, her twisted hair flowing perfectly behind her. With the sunset behind her she looks like a painting, or an illustration in the Peter Pan book. The other sound gets louder. What *is* it?

Oh. It's dogs barking.

I sit up to say something, do something, but it's too late.

There's a rush and a roar. The water near the rock swirls in a circle, strong, like there's a tornado under the water. Jasmina's voice cracks as something breaks through the surface.

I scream so hard it feels like I'm tearing my throat.

There's a monster. Right in front of us.

The top is a woman, with a beautiful, mermaid-like face, though her long hair writhes strangely. It looks like it's made of eels, constantly slithering around her head. Her bottom half is tentacles like an octopus's, coiling under her, pushing her up through the water. She's massive, ten or eleven feet high, blocking the sun.

But what makes me scream most is her middle. Around her waist, coming right out of her skin all the way around, is a pack of barking, braying dogs. The front halves of dogs, five or six of them. They're frantic and wild, their mouths snapping in the air, their paws wheeling. The monster lunges for the mermaid and in one movement grabs her, throws her over one shoulder, and dives back below the waves.

The barking lasts for a few seconds; then everything is quiet and still. The water is smooth again.

I press my hand over my mouth, hard. I don't think we're going to win this adventure. If that's our foe, it's nothing we're going to be able to fight.

"What was that?" Shoe asks, her voice a squeak.

"You don't know?" I whisper, like if I'm too loud the monster will come back. "She hasn't been here before?"

Shoe shakes her head.

"That's way worse than the dragon," Rella says. Tears shine in her eyes. "It's terrible."

All the mermaids cluster in a tight huddle in the middle of the lagoon. It looks like they've never seen this creature before either. The Lost Boys just stand there in shock—even Peter. We have to do something, right? But what can we do?

Peter runs down to talk to the mermaids. The rest of the Lost Boys gather in groups, whispering to each other. I can see them miming the eels, the dogs. I shudder.

Fergus's fingers are tapping, and he's breathing fast. I'm not sure he's verbal right now—when he's really upset or overwhelmed, sometimes he loses his speech.

But he slides his backpack off, unzips it, and pulls out one of his mythology books. He bends over it, studying the index, then thumbs to a page and hands the book to me.

It's the story of Scylla and Charybdis. I don't remember him telling me about this one before, but it's from *The Odyssey,* so I'm sure he knows it pretty well. I read. Scylla is a monster in Greek mythology who killed six of the men on Odysseus's ship, snatching them right off the ship and eating them. Odysseus couldn't defeat her. Later Hercules killed her . . . but her father, a god, brought her back to life. It doesn't say what happened after that. She's half woman, half octopus . . . with barking dogs around her middle.

"Oh no," I whisper. I look at Fergus. "This is who that was? Did we bring her somehow?"

Fergus nods solemnly.

"But she's a myth!" Myths are supposed to be pretend. They're scary, but they're still just stories.

That was real. There wasn't any pretend to that monster. I keep forgetting we're *in* a story. But this isn't the fun Neverland adventure I was expecting.

Fergus sits down next to me, locking his arms tight around his knees.

"Are you okay?" I ask.

He doesn't answer. I want to help him calm down, like I usually do. But all the things I would normally say—don't worry, we can fix this, I can take care of it—none of them fit. We *should* worry. And if that's a myth, he knows more about this than I do, than any of us do.

I look at Peter, standing with his ankles in the water. We're going to have to tell him about Scylla.

Fergus

I can't talk. It's like my brain overloaded looking at the monster, and it burned out the part where I can get words from my head to my mouth. But I know who that is.

I know who that is.

That has to be Scylla, here in the flesh. From my books. I know the story well.

Scylla was a nymph, the daughter of Phorcys and Hecate. She was young and beautiful, and Glaucus, a sea god, fell in love with her.

That's never good.

She refused Glaucus—I think because he had a tail—

119

and ran away. But Glaucus wouldn't take no for an answer. He went to Circe, the famous witch, and asked for a love potion so Scylla would fall in love with him back. But Circe fell in love with Glaucus—so instead of a love potion, she secretly gave him a poison, and told him to pour it into the pool where Scylla bathed. He did, and it turned Scylla into a monster. Then Glaucus ran away from *her*.

Scylla was left alone, a terrible monster, and she didn't even do anything wrong. Glaucus seeing her, and being interested in her, ruined her whole life. In some of the books she has seven heads, or a snake tail, or three rows of teeth. But here she looks like some of the other drawings I've seen, with the tentacles and the human top . . . and always, always, there are the dogs, alive, coming right out of her skin.

She's *here*. Somehow I brought a monster to Neverland just by knowing about it.

I need to be alone for a while, to think things through. I wave at Clover to stay where she is and then go up the path a little, behind a bush with big, flat leaves. It's out of sight of everyone. I sit on the ground, pull my knees up, shut my eyes, and rock.

It's calm, quiet. I can hear the ocean murmuring against the shore, see the stars getting bright overhead.

We've only been here for one day, I realize. All that happened in one day.

I rock back and forth, using the same rhythm as the waves in the ocean. It's soothing, and I can control it, which helps. I breathe, slow and deep. Suddenly I feel warmth in front of me, by my chest.

I open my eyes. One of the pixies is there, snuggled as close as she can be without quite touching. The light is brilliant. Warmth pulses from her, matching my rhythm, my heartbeat. She's helping. It reminds me of a cat purring, snuggled up in your lap. It's the same feeling.

I fumble my voice recorder out of my pocket, go back to track fourteen, and press Play. Mom's voice comes out, talking about breakfast. I recorded her the day before we left. "Would you like strawberries today, Fergus?" she asks, and my eyes fill up. I rewind and play it again. "Would you like strawberries today, Fergus?"

There's someone else here too now, a more solid presence. I know without looking that it's Clover. She sits there for a while, silent, and that helps too. After I repeat Mom a few more times, I hit Stop.

"We can go back, if you want," she whispers.

The pixie flies straight up and away. I clutch my chest, missing where it was. But I think my mouth might work now. "Back?" I ask.

Clover brushes her hair off her face. "To London. We can make them take us back."

I hadn't even considered that. I think about it. It's scary being here, if we have to face a real monster. Scylla is a serious monster. But we knew there would be adventure coming in. There's always adventure in Neverland. And I think of running up the trail, laughing, splashing the others, singing the marching song. Dancing on top of the mountain. Sitting by the fire with everyone.

I don't have to worry all the time here about whether I'm bothering people. No one stares, or looks at me funny. Ever.

I'm not ready to give that up. And if Scylla is here because I'm here . . .

"We need to stay," I say firmly. "Help."

Clover scrunches up her face like she does when she's thinking, but then she nods. "I showed Peter the part in the book about Scylla, but he and the Lost Boys are waiting for you. They want you to tell them more about her. Are you okay to do that?"

I close my eyes, to gather myself. "More time."

We sit for a while longer. I listen to the ocean, and think about Mom making breakfast, about the rhythm of the waves. My brain starts to come back together, untangling.

I think I'm ready to go now.

We go back to the group—sitting together on the beach, silent—and I tell them everything I know about Scylla. I read them passages from my books. They listen, still quiet, and then Peter goes to tell the mermaids.

He comes back frowning, which looks wrong on his face. "We know who she is, thanks to Fergus. But why is she stealing the mermaids?"

"Maybe they made her jealous," Friendly adds. "Because she used to be like them."

There's silence for a while. That's a good idea. Then Clover clears her throat. "The song?" Clover asks softly. "Maybe it was bothering her? Or called her?"

Peter's face lights up. "The song. Or the songs. You sang first, Clover, and your song called me, in London. Maybe your song called this Scylla monster, and then when Jasmina started singing, Scylla took her."

Clover frowns hard, the worry lines deep in her forehead. "Wait. *My* song?" she whispers.

"I know what to do," Peter says, triumphant. He jumps to his feet. "Clover, you can go out on the rock—the mermaids can take you out, if you can't swim—"

"I can swim," Clover breaks in. "But—"

"I will be there too, on the rock with you. You will sing. Then when Scylla comes up, I will slay her. Cut her head off. Easy!" He mimes slicing with a sword. "Then the mermaids can swim down to her lair, wherever that

123

is, and find Jasmina and Allora and rescue them. It will be a great victory. *Peter Pan versus the Sea Monster!*" He turns to me. "You can put it in a book, and everyone will tell the story." He rubs his hands together, grinning. "We'll have to do it tomorrow, when the sun's up. I will go tell the mermaids."

He runs down to the shore again. The Lost Boys start cheering, like we've already won.

But my chest is twisted into knots of anxiety. "Clover?" I whisper. "That isn't safe."

I look up and meet her eyes, and I can name that emotion. She looks terrified.

Clover

I can't do this.

I think it over and over. I can't say it out loud, not even to Fergus.

We're on the beach again, the sun just up, waiting for Peter to make the call to go. Fergus is talking to Friendly, discussing strategy, and the others seem more excited than nervous. I sit by myself, panicking.

How can I stand out on the rock and sing, knowing it might bring that monster right to me? What if Peter can't kill it, and it really drags me down under the water? I'm not a mermaid. I'll drown. I'll *die*.

The Lost Boys say Peter never loses, that there's

nothing to be afraid of. He was pretty impressive with the mountain lion, and in the story he's fearless against Captain Hook. But he's never faced this monster before. He's never *seen* this monster before. None of them have.

And I bet Wendy was still afraid when she was going to have to walk the plank.

What would Wendy do? She was my great-great-grandmother, after all. She did well here. I can try to be like her.

She was brave, for sure. She took care of her little brothers *and* all the Lost Boys. I bet she'd swim right out there and sing.

But she was also always worrying about risks . . . so maybe she wouldn't. Maybe she'd put her hands on her hips and say, "This is ridiculous! Think of something else!"

I know Mom would say it's ridiculous. I can hear her in my head. *Be safe, Clover,* she'd say. This is far from safe.

They're depending on me—the mermaids, the Lost Boys, Fergus . . . everyone.

But I can't do this.

"Are you okay?" Shoe asks. She drops on the sand next to me. I braided her hair again this morning, in two

French braids, and she's super pleased with it. She tugs on the ends and studies me, her dark eyes calm.

I feel like I can trust her, of all of them. I swallow. "I can't do it," I say.

"Sing to bring the monster?" Her eyes don't change, still relaxed. "You'll be safe. Peter always wins."

"So you'd do it?"

"Of course!" She stretches out her legs and leans back. "I was bait for a bear once. I had to sit very quietly with a fish in my lap and wait for it to come close enough for Peter to shoot it with an arrow." She frowns. "Thinking about it now, I don't know why we couldn't have just left the fish. But it was scary sitting there. When the bear came to the clearing, it roared so loud I shook, and I wanted to jump up and run, right into the sea. But Peter shot it in time. You must trust him." She opens her arms wide, gesturing to the beach, the whole island. "Neverland is his place. You do not need to worry." She smiles. Her teeth are crooked, but they fit her. "You worry too much."

I smile back, small. I feel a tiny bit better. "Yeah. Probably."

I just have to trust that this really is Peter's place, and he's not going to let me get taken by a monster.

"It's time!" Peter calls. "Let's go!"

Oh God. It's time.

I stand on the edge of the beach, my toes in the foam, breathing in the familiar salt smell of the ocean. It's not soothing at all anymore.

Serena and the other mermaids did some exploring on their own, underwater, but they haven't been able to find anything. Serena thinks Scylla and the mermaids might be hidden with magic, and when Scylla dies, the mermaids will be released.

I take a deep breath and look over my shoulder at Fergus. He's standing apart from everyone else, rubbing his mouth. I'd nod to him, or smile bravely or something, like people do in movies—but he's not looking at me. And I don't feel brave anyway.

I run my hands over the "swimming suit." Shoe lent it to me, since it would be pretty nasty to swim in jeans. It's mostly a band on the top, with improvised straps tied on, and loose shorts. It's dark brown and green, and doesn't fit very well, but at least it's made of bits of cloth. I was afraid the leaf clothes that some of them wear might just dissolve in the water after a while.

I feel naked without my backpack. I wish I could take it with me.

"Away we go!" Peter calls, and dives into the water,

his sword sheathed in a long stripe at his back. The Lost Boys cheer. I look at Shoe, and she smiles and nods. I guess I can't wait any longer. I take a step, then two, the water swirling cool against my ankles. The bottom drops off, and suddenly there's nothing beneath my feet. I splutter for a second, but then a hand takes mine, and I get my balance. Serena is with me.

We swim together all the way to the rock. The water is the perfect temperature against my skin, the sun warm but not too bright, the waves relaxing, not too strong. It would be wonderful, if I weren't swimming to face a terrible monster. I don't want to get out of the water, but Serena lets go of my hand, and Peter reaches down and takes it, pulling me up onto the rock. It's warm and smooth against my bare feet.

I look back at the beach, at the line of Lost Boys waving and cheering. They seem far away. Fergus is still rubbing his mouth.

I can't do this. I can't. I can't call a monster.

"Get your breath," Peter says, "then sing!"

His voice is excited, but still calm. Like he's really in control. *Trust Peter,* Shoe said.

What would Wendy do? Well, this far into the plan, I'm pretty sure she would sing. She'd lift her chin and get it done. She'd have to.

I guess I have to.

Peter pulls his sword out of the sheath, with a strange swooshing sound, and stands close to me, ready.

I look at Fergus one more time, wipe my hands on my wet shorts, and sing.

Fergus

Clover is singing "Alouette"—but I can't watch, and I can't even really listen. It feels like my heart is beating in my throat instead of my chest, and it's beating wrong. Jerking. I can't stop rubbing my mouth, but it doesn't help. I still feel the panic.

What if she's taken? What if she dies? Clover is sometimes annoying, and always worries, and makes me do things when I don't want to . . . but she's my sister. I need her.

Mom wouldn't have let her do this. I shouldn't have let her.

"Alouette, gentille alouette . . ." Her voice reaches out

through the air, the words curling around me. I can easily believe Scylla would come to her voice.

But Scylla doesn't come. Clover's in the third verse, and there's nothing. I start to relax a little. Maybe she won't come. Maybe she wanted two mermaids and that was all. I dare to peek.

Clover looks brave, standing there on the rock, singing with her hands in fists. I've seen that expression before, usually when she's standing up for me when someone is being a bully. Peter seems ready next to her, with his sword drawn.

I relax more, the pressure releasing. It'll be okay. Scylla won't come, and Clover will swim back, and we'll find the monster another way. Or maybe never see her again.

"Je te plumerai le cou, je te plumerai le cou . . ."

That part means "I'll pluck the feathers off your neck." I almost feel like laughing.

The water churns, and the dogs bark in the distance. Oh no.

Scylla is coming.

I want to look away, but I can't. I need to be strong for Clover. If she can do this, I can watch. Even though my whole body is trembling.

"Be okay, be okay, be okay," I chant under my breath. The dogs are loud, close. Clover's voice has gotten so quiet I can barely hear it, but I see her mouth moving. The water looks like it's boiling. Peter takes a fighting stance. He seems excited, not scared.

The Lost Boys are all silent now, watching with me.

Scylla breaks the surface, and I can't move an inch. She looks bigger than before, terrifying. Those dogs could tear someone apart. She lunges out of the water and goes straight for Clover. Peter leaps in front of her, slashing with his sword. He gets a hit, blood streaming down Scylla's arm.

Scylla stops, pulls back, and eyes Peter. But she doesn't study him like he's a fearsome opponent. More like he's a bug in her way. Peter still doesn't seem afraid; he's ready with the sword again. Clover is hiding behind him, so I can't see her very well.

Peter strikes, but misses.

Suddenly Scylla reaches out, grabs Peter with one hand, and flings him away, sword and all, into the ocean, far outside the lagoon.

The Lost Boys shout in horror. One of the mermaids streaks off after him.

I really can't breathe, my throat clamped in panic. Clover is alone. She's defenseless against a hideous killer sea monster. She's like Andromeda in *Clash of the Titans*. A helpless sacrifice.

Clover shrinks down against the rock, covering her head with her arms.

Scylla reaches out, snatches Clover off the rock, and throws her over her shoulder. Then she spins, and dives back down into the water.

I find enough breath to scream, and sink to my knees in the sand.

I'm frozen. A statue. I can't think, or move. Clover's underwater. She'll drown if she's underwater for too long. How long does it take to drown? I don't think I want to know.

Two of the mermaids dive after them. Maybe they can rescue Clover. Maybe they can win against Scylla.

But Scylla is a goddess and a monster. She flicked Peter Pan away like he was a piece of fluff. What can the mermaids do? What can any of us do?

Tears pour down my face. This is shock, grief. I know the words, but I didn't understand before.

Clover is gone. Clover is *gone*.

Friendly, George, and Jumper come hover around me, their worried faces making it worse. I want to run away and scream again, let out all these terrible feelings. Shoe sits next to me and puts her arms around me. I pull away—it's too much—but she stays there nearby, crouched on the sand.

"Serena's coming back with Peter!" Rella calls. Everyone but Friendly and Shoe runs to look, shading their eyes with their hands. I can see them, barely, two bright blobs in the water heading this way.

Friendly touches my shoulder. "I'm sorry," he says gently. "We'll get her back. We always get hostages back."

"She'll drown!" I say. It comes out like a howl.

"Probably not," he says. "It's magic, after all. Everything here is magic one way or another."

I don't know if I believe him anymore.

"I told her to go," Shoe says to Friendly. Her voice is shaky. "I told her it would be safe."

"She'll be okay," Friendly says. "We always get hostages back."

I'm breathing too fast. My head feels light, like it's going to float away.

The Lost Boys meet Peter at the shore, but he strides through them, straight toward me. His face is tomato red, freckles popping out all over his cheeks. His real color has gone dark green, the color of the forest in shadow.

I push to my feet. I want to be standing when I face him.

"This is your fault!" I yell, before he even reaches

me. "You said you could defeat her! You said Clover would be safe!"

The Lost Boys circle around us, and two pixies flutter right by Peter's ear. The red spreads down his neck, and I think he's going to yell back at me or hit me or something. But he presses his lips together, tight, and then he nods.

"You are right. I thought I could defeat her, but I have not faced any such as her before. I went in unprepared, and she has Clover because of it. I . . . I apologize."

A couple of the Lost Boys gasp. I guess Peter hasn't apologized much before.

What good does it do, though? Clover is still gone.

Clover

She threw Peter. Threw him right into the ocean. Then she turned her eyes on me, and I knew it was over. There wasn't going to be a safe, triumphant return to the beach, a victory in our adventure before we go back to London.

We lost. And now I'm drowning.

I can't see anything. My throat tightens, and I'm not sure I could breathe if I wanted to. I kick, and flail my arms. There's nothing but water everywhere. Something cold and slimy slides across my bare back, and I realize it's one of the eels that are Scylla's hair.

I can't believe this is the way it happens. Drowned by a sea monster.

Scylla stops, as suddenly as if we've come to the end of a line. She flips me off her shoulder with one hand and holds me out in front of her, studying me.

I squirm, trying desperately to gasp for air. There is no air.

"You are not a water creature," she says. Her voice is rough and low—it echoes around me, in my head, in the water. "You are a land girl. Interesting. I was a land girl once. I will give you the gift."

As quick as a finger snap, the pressure is gone. I try to take a breath, and somehow—though it's water around me and not air—it works. I can breathe.

The fear flies away, replaced by a strange exhilaration. I can breathe underwater. I'm not going to drown. I can *breathe.*

I can see again too, as clearly as if I were looking at the water through glass. I see Scylla's face plainly for the first time. Her eyes are bright green, with gray circles under them. She looks tired. She has a long nose, like on Greek statues, and pale white skin you can almost see through.

Scylla throws me over her shoulder again and dives, fast. It's so fast the ocean is a blur, my hair flying behind me.

The dogs are still barking, their barks echoing like

Scylla's voice. They're not far from my head, which is bouncing on Scylla's back. The closest one—a brown dog with smooth, short fur—snaps at me, but it can't quite reach.

I wonder if they bark constantly.

The color changes below us, and I think we're coming close to the seafloor. I see coral, and rocks, and things skittering along the bottom. Scylla turns and swims parallel to the ground. I can't see where we're going, but she does three twisty turns, as rocks fly past, and then stops suddenly again. She waves her hands, mutters something, and we pass through a curtain of kelp, into a sort of undersea house in a cave, with a high roof.

Scylla sets me down gently on a rock that's shaped like a chair and studies me, the eels whipping around her head, the dogs snapping. I grip the arms of the chair, cold and hard. If I didn't hold on, I think I'd just float up again.

"I must secure the boundary. I will return. Do not move." She glares at me. "Or you will be very sorry."

She swims back out the entrance, and the sound of the dogs fades. I let go of the chair and float up to the middle of the room. I look around quickly. This may be my only chance to escape.

It's beautiful, in the same otherworldly way the

pixies' houses were beautiful. There's a main room, where I am, and then two more kelp curtains, which I guess lead to other rooms. There are no windows to escape through, unfortunately. There are three other chairs spread around the room. The chairs are deep, so Scylla could probably perch on them to rest, in spite of the dogs. A wide, high table stands in the middle, carved out of a massive rock. But what makes this place beautiful are the decorations—the art.

The ceiling, which arches high above me, is completely covered in a mural made of some sort of phosphorescent paint that glows in the dark space. It looks like a drawing from one of the mythology books: a flowing river, with a merman popping out of it, holding out his arms to a young woman on the shore who's running away. I know what it is, from Fergus's story: that's Scylla running away, before she becomes a monster. And Glaucus, who started all of this.

The walls are decorated with shells, all different sizes and colors, stuck on in detailed patterns. Some are only patterns, I think, but some are in the shapes of flowers, rainbows. A fire, dancing. A giant tree spreading its branches. They're all painted with that glowing stuff too, so the whole room is bright enough to see pretty well.

I move to the entrance—I really have to go before

she comes back. But as soon as my hand touches the empty space, it's zapped, with an intense, burning pain. I cry out.

One of the kelp curtains moves, and a face peeks around it. It's Jasmina. I recognize her from that first day on the beach. I see another face over her shoulder, pale and scared. That must be Allora.

"You're alive!" My voice echoes, like Scylla's did.

"You can breathe!" Jasmina says, her eyebrows knotting together. "How?"

"Scylla—the sea monster—said she gave me the gift of breath," I say. "I don't know how I can talk, either, but it seems to work. Are you both all right?"

She nods. "We cannot leave this room. She has locked the entrance with magic." She stretches her hand out an inch past the curtain, then snatches it back like it was burned. "She has not harmed us . . . yet. But we must find a way to leave this place as soon as we can."

"But what does she want?"

"She is returning!" Jasmina says, and drops the curtain.

I shoot back through the water to the seat, my heart pounding. Sure enough, I hear the dogs first; then Scylla appears. She glances around the room, then at me. She frowns, showing two deep lines in her forehead.

"What did you do?" she booms.

"Nothing!" I whisper. She comes closer, the dogs lunging at me, tumbling over each other. I close my eyes. "I looked around," I say, my voice high. I don't want to get the mermaids in trouble too, so I don't say anything about them. "That's all. I was looking at the ceiling. It's . . . it's beautiful."

Scylla studies me. "You cannot escape with flattery. It is an old mortal's trick, and I know it well." She sighs. "I have seen it used on others."

I grip the chair, looking up at her, at the eels and the dogs.

She flicks an eel off her shoulder irritably. "There is no one following you. I have secured our area. No one will find us now."

"What do you want?" I ask. I see Allora and Jasmina peeking around the curtain again. "Why did you bring us here?"

My voice hardly shakes at all, but it's only bluffing. I'm terrified.

She frowns. "Are you slow as well as mortal? I want you to sing."

20

Fergus

No one is doing anything.

Actually, they're doing their normal things. Peter sent us all back to the house to rest and "regroup." He stayed with the mermaids, so I think at least maybe he's making a plan. The two mermaids who followed Scylla and Clover said they saw what looked like an underwater house, but they couldn't get near it. And Clover appeared to be breathing underwater.

How could she be breathing underwater?

I feel like *I* still can't breathe right. Agitation jumps under my skin like electricity. But at the same time I'm too upset to even scream. It's more like everything has shut down. My body and my brain aren't working at all.

I go stand in one of the tree passageways for a while, where it's cool and dark and tight. It's hard to explain why a tight space helps—especially since I don't like hugs or people touching me—but pressure, or a small, confined area, just makes me feel better. More in control. My thoughts settle a little, from a brain whirl to a tumble, and I can breathe.

Feeling better won't get Clover back, though. I have to think of a way to save her.

What are the facts? She's underwater. With a monster. A monster *I* brought here. We can't reach her. We can't defeat Scylla easily—Peter tried that and failed.

I have to do something. I can't just sit around and let Clover be down there with a monster who might eat her.

I go and wait up above, in the clearing. When Peter comes back, I lunge at him. "What's the plan?" I ask. "We need a plan. What's the plan?"

He still doesn't look as worried as I want him to be.

"What's the *plan*?" I repeat.

He drops his head and runs a hand through his hair. "Nothing yet. It's deep, far too deep for us to swim. And she's powerful. There aren't enough mermaids to defeat her." He shrugs, and tries a smile. "We'll think of something. It'll work out, you'll see. We'll eat supper in an hour or two, and you can tell us all the stories you know of Scylla again. There will be a clue in there as to how she can be defeated." The smile drops, and his voice gets quieter. "Neverland always gives us clues."

The words sound sure, but he doesn't look as confident as he normally does. We believed Peter would protect Clover on the rock, because the Lost Boys said it was safe. Because Peter always wins in the stories. That's how it should have happened, if it was a story in a book. Peter would've killed the monster, saved Clover, and we'd be done. Safe, with a good story to tell when we got home.

What's wrong with our story? Why isn't it working? Is the Greek myth I brought with me stronger than Neverland?

Peter looks around the clearing. "Are you on guard? Good. I need a nap before supper."

He disappears below, and I'm left alone again. Naps. Food. Stories. What I want is *action*.

I fetch my books. Maybe Peter's right. Maybe the clue is in the stories, and I want to find it.

★ ✷ ★

Two wasted hours later—after supper and naps—I sit in the clearing, with my books in my lap, and tell everyone all the stories about Scylla again.

It would be fun to tell stories to the Lost Boys if Clover were here. Even though I'm saying serious things, everyone oohs and aahs at the descriptions and the heroes. They all listen to me with wide eyes, like I'm special because I know the stories. I don't think anyone has looked at me that way before. No one has ever listened to me so intently.

Good. They need to know every detail if we're going to get my sister back.

"'Scylla is not of mortal kind,'" I say, quoting Circe from *The Odyssey*. "'She is grim and baleful, savage, not to be wrestled with. Against her there is no defense, and the best path is the path of flight.'"

Run away, because she's immortal and impossible to defeat. When I say that line, even Peter looks bleak. Captain Hook at least was mortal.

"We can't kill her, then," Friendly says. Pixie light flickers on his face, on all their faces, as the pixies dart around the circle.

"Can't kill her," I repeat, and look at the ground. "Can't kill her," I whisper. Because it's true, and I don't know what else to say.

There's silence for a long time. Nothing but the insects in the trees, the calls of birds. I hum and stare at my book, the words jumping back and forth. I could read more, but that really is all there is to say. And I think I'm done talking.

"If we can't kill the monster," Shoe says slowly, "we need to get her to leave somehow."

No one answers, but Peter nods. I hum in agreement. I don't think anyone hears me. After a little while, Shoe goes on.

"It would help to understand why she's here . . . or, if it's only because Fergus and Clover are here, why she's taken some of the mermaids. What does she want? We know she didn't kill them—right away at least . . ." She gulps. "So it's not for food or just killing."

I shudder.

"It was the singing that brought her up, that brought her to the mermaids and Clover," George says.

"Right," Friendly agrees. "We knew that. So it must be something to do with the singing. Either she wants to stop it, or she wants more of it."

"Maybe she just wants them to sing to her," I say. "She was a nymph before, a long time ago, and we don't know where she's been since Hercules killed her. Maybe she misses singing."

"Or maybe she wants them to sing for some specific reason," Peter adds. "That's why she took them with her."

I nod, excited that we're finally getting somewhere. Singing has to be the key—all of them were taken while they were singing, so it must be that.

But she is still a monster, and I know what monsters do, from all the stories. A chill like ice water splashes down my spine.

"She might kill them still." I say it out loud so everyone else will know it too. "Even if this is all true. She is a monster and a Greek goddess. She might kill them if they don't sing the way she wants. She might already have done it."

There's only silence after that. I look up at the trees, listen to a bird squawking, and wish that I could scream and scream and that would fix everything.

Or that Clover were here to make me feel better.

I grit my teeth. She isn't dead. She isn't. And I'll find a way to get her back.

Clover

Scylla studies me so intently that I start to wonder if she has X-ray vision or something, like she can see through to my thoughts. The dogs bark and bark.

"You want us to sing?" I squeak, because it feels like I have to say something, and I don't want her thinking about how I disobeyed her.

She makes a sound of disgust and turns away, swimming across to the room where Allora and Jasmina are. She places one hand in front of the door, closes her eyes, and says a few words, too low to hear. "You may come forth," she says. They swim out and stay awkwardly by the table.

"Clover!" Jasmina says, sounding shocked, as though we haven't just spoken. "Are you all right?"

"I'm Allora," Allora says behind her. "Jasmina told me about you and your brother."

Allora is smaller than Jasmina, curvier. Her light blond hair is loose, fanning around her face in the water.

Scylla's head jerks from them to me, her eyes narrow. I swear she knows we talked already.

"Hello. I'm . . . I'm okay," I say. "I think."

Scylla takes one of the deep seats, gingerly, the dogs still scrabbling with their paws and barking. Always barking. I try not to look at the dogs directly, in case it's rude.

"Sit," Scylla says to Allora and Jasmina. She points at the chairs. "I must tell this land girl my story, since she is too stupid to figure it out herself."

"I know some of it," I say, stung. I'm not stupid. She raises her eyebrows, and the eels swish around wildly on her head. Maybe I shouldn't have spoken, but it's too late now. "My brother told me. You're Scylla. Glaucus fell in love with you, but you rejected him. And then Circe turned you into . . . into . . ."

"A monster." She sighs. "I accept the word. It is not a kind or gentle descriptor, but I am neither kind nor gentle, not anymore. I have eaten men whole. I have torn them apart, with my dogs. In the early years as a *monster* I was very angry, bitter toward all mankind, and I was not merciful." She leans back in the chair, and two of the dogs yelp reproachfully. She sits up again.

I think of her tearing men apart and eating them *whole*. I grip the arms of my chair hard.

"But after I was killed by the mortal hero and my father brought me back to life," Scylla continues, "I wanted no more of that. No more of people or their hatred for me. My father built me this cave and hid it away, far in the depths of the ocean. From that day to . . . not long ago, I was alone. I spent my time making art." She gestures to the roof, the walls. "I would have been at peace if not for the dogs."

"They do bark a great deal," Jasmina says flatly.

Scylla closes her eyes, then opens them again. The lines in her face look deep in the half-light. "They bark endlessly. When one goes hoarse, another picks it up, stronger. I cannot sleep. I have not slept more than a few minutes in a thousand years."

I groan in sympathy. I'm terrible when I don't get a full night's sleep, because of worrying too much. I can't imagine *never* sleeping. For an eternity.

Scylla stares at the ceiling, her eyes empty. The dogs bark. And bark. And bark.

The rest of us are quiet.

"Not long ago I heard the singing—that one

singing." Scylla points at Allora. "It came down through the ocean, beautiful and strange. I had not heard singing since I was a nymph. I had not heard any other beings at all, deep in my hidden cave. But with the singing, two of the dogs began to fall asleep." She shrugs her shoulders, like it's a mystery. "I swam up to the surface and found that my cave is no longer where it was, but in an odd and different land. I took the singer so she could sing for me whenever I wanted."

Allora glares at the rocky floor, her expression grim.

"But only two of the dogs slept. It did not help, not enough. Later the singing came again. That one." Scylla points at Jasmina. "Two more of the dogs dozed off. So I took her, too, to make them sing together. It is a relief, but still, *still* I cannot sleep."

Her X-ray gaze turns to me. "I know your singing was a trap for me. I have lived through many mortals' traps. I could have just let you be, or killed you, like I have killed others." She rests her hand on one of the dog's heads, but it snaps at her. I don't move, don't say anything. "I could have thrown you into the ocean, like I threw your hero, Pan. But your singing—it lulled the last two dogs. I needed you. I need you. All three of you, to sing my dogs to sleep. To give me rest."

Allora shifts, gripping the edge of the table like it's

152

the only thing keeping her from running away. What has it been like down here with Scylla?

Scylla stares up at the ceiling again. "You may ask your question, land girl," she says, almost bored. "I see you have one."

I frown. "I understand," I say quietly. "I get why you did it, why you brought us here. But what happens if it works, if our singing lets you finally sleep?"

"Then you will stay with me here," Scylla says, like it's obvious. Her gaze snaps back to me. "Forever."

Fergus

It's darker in Neverland than I've ever seen it back home. In San Diego there are so many lights: house lights, streetlights, all the businesses and people who never seem to sleep. I've tried to look at the stars before, to see Andromeda and Aries and Hercules in the sky, but there's too much distraction, too much light pollution. I've found Cassiopeia and Orion, but the rest are too hard to pick out without going to the observatory. And that's not the same as seeing them with your own eyes. Here it's so dark you can see everything.

All the Lost Boys were snoring, but I couldn't sleep. It felt wrong, anyway, to lie down like there's nothing the matter, when Clover was here last night and now she's not.

I've never been alone outside at night before. I'm hardly ever alone outside at all, to be honest. Mom or Clover or someone is always around to make sure that I'm okay, that I don't need something. That I don't run into other people, or wander away, or have a meltdown.

It feels free to be by myself, to not have anyone even know where I am. I can't scream or sing, because I'd wake everyone up, but I can do anything quiet. I can spin. I can make my hands fly. I can rock. I can make all the faces I want. I try one to see what it feels like, a fearsome frowning face, but then it feels like I'm forgetting Clover is with a monster right now, so I stop.

But I'm too restless to stay here by the house. And there are still too many trees for me to see all the stars.

I could go for a walk up the mountain—up there I could see the whole sky. And maybe . . . maybe I could see where Clover is, find some clue that no one else has noticed, from way up at the top. Maybe I can do something to make it all right again. I have to do *something*.

I'll be back before they even wake up.

I take the left path out of the woods, the one that doesn't go through the Haunted Forest or Pixie Hollow. It goes around the base of the mountain, then through to the other side and up, eventually joining the path with the waterfall.

I'm not afraid. I can't name all the feelings that are in my chest, but fear isn't one of them. Clover faced the sea monster, on purpose, and she got taken below the waves. I can go for a hike, even in solid dark. Even by myself.

Something crackles behind me, a person or animal in the brush, and the insect sounds cut off. I stop and listen.

In Wendy's time, at least in the movie, that could've been a pirate. Here I don't know what it could be: the mountain lion again, or a dragon, or a deer. I wait, quiet, my hands tapping silently on my leg, until the insects start up again. They know when it's safe.

I keep going, out of the trees, on the flat dirt path along the bottom of the mountain. From here you can't see the lagoons. I can see the ocean, or at least hear it—a flat darkness that murmurs back and forth against the sand. The smell of salt and seaweed is strong in my nose.

How could Clover be out there? How could she not be dead, under the waves?

How do I know she's not dead?

I don't. But I don't believe it.

I stop and look at the stars. From here a lot of them are still hidden behind the mountain, and they're all in different places than at home. But I see Orion's familiar belt. And then I see Andromeda.

Andromeda in the stories was chained to a rock to face a sea monster, the Kraken. She faced it like Clover did—but she was expected to die, a sacrifice. Perseus saved her by showing Medusa's head to the Kraken and turning him into stone. That's in *Clash of the Titans*.

I can't do that for Clover. I can't hunt down Medusa, who's already dead. I can't turn Scylla into stone. But I have to be like Perseus and think of a different way to save her.

I keep walking, the ocean on my left. The path starts to tilt up, and I stumble. It's hard to see my feet in the dark. I should've brought the flashlight that's in my backpack, still in the underground house. I didn't think of that.

Suddenly the ground brightens, like a flashlight is pointing at it. I look up, startled, and see that a pixie has joined me. I don't know which one, of course, but I imagine it's the same one that comforted me at the beach, that felt like a warm, purring cat. I smile, though I don't know what that looks like to a pixie.

"Hello," I say. The pixie circles around me once, fast,

and then goes back to its place near my knees, lighting the way. I wish I knew what the pixie's name was, but I guess it doesn't matter. I'm not that good with remembering names anyway. Sometimes I see someone I know, and all I can remember is the first letter of their name, but nothing else. It's like all names in my brain are organized in boxes by letter, but sometimes when I go to find the detail, the box is locked.

Pixie will do, for now.

The path dives into a tunnel that goes through to the other side of the mountain, and now I'm really glad Pixie is here. I thought outside was dark, but inside the tunnel it's so black the darkness feels solid, alive. A different monster. I wouldn't even be able to see my hand if the pixie light weren't shining. It's quiet in here too, without the sound of the ocean or the birds or insects. There's only a steady drip, drip of water down the walls.

Pixie stops. I take a step farther, then another, but Pixie darts in front of me and nudges against my knees, pushing me back.

"Hello?" I whisper. "Is something there?"

Pixie waits for a minute, like it's making sure I won't move, then darts forward, its light bobbing higher. Something swishes. And then I see.

There's a low overhang, the bottom of it even with the middle of my forehead. If I'd kept walking I would've slammed right into it and probably knocked myself out.

There's also a line of bats hanging from their feet by the stone ceiling. I see them on the low part and, when Pixie flies higher, all the way around. Hundreds of furry little bodies, red eyes winking in the light.

A thrill of fear runs through me, but I squash it. I learned about bats at the zoo in San Diego, in one of their school programs. They look scary, but most of them eat fruit. They're not a threat. I shouldn't be afraid of them at all.

"Why are you here, bats?" I whisper. "Shouldn't you be out hunting right now, when it's nice and dark?"

As if in answer, every bat in the cave moves at once, in a rush, shooting past me in a rustling cloud. I squat down, my arms covering my head, but I still feel the breeze of all their wings on my face, my hair. The pixie curls up close to my chest. We hang on, still, like fish in the middle of a stream. I imitate the whooshing sound as best I can, closing my eyes. *Whooosh. Whooosh.*

We wait until they're all gone, all quiet except the drip, and then I monster-walk under the overhang and stand up again. From here I can see the faint light of the other end of the tunnel, and I can go fast. When we come out of the cave it seems lighter, with more stars. I can hear the waterfall above me, the pounding water.

I hear something else, too, from somewhere far out in the deep of the ocean.

Barking.

Clover

Scylla gives us food, to give us strength before we sing, but I can't eat it. The giant blue platter is full of snails—still crawling around, still with their shells on—and kelp, just plucked from the ocean, weighed down with stones. Allora and Jasmina eat hungrily, plucking the snails out of the shells and swallowing them in one gulp.

I pick at the kelp, but it just tastes like raw, wet spinach. It makes me gag. It also makes me aware again that there's water in my mouth, and I'm swallowing it all the time somehow without drowning. I don't know how, except that it's Scylla's magic.

I set the kelp down on the platter, back under the stone, and see Scylla watching me.

"I will find something for you to eat, land girl," she says kindly. The eels writhe around her head. "Even if I have to fetch it from the island. I remember, faintly, the taste of fruit."

"You could bring me up to the island," I say hopefully, "and I could get food for myself."

She sighs and leans back, the dogs yelping again. "And I would see you no more, and I still would not have sleep. I am a goddess and a monster, but no fool. I know all the tricks of mortals, and some of the tricks of gods. You would be wise to remember that."

It would have been too easy, I guess. My stomach growls, but there's nothing I can do about it now, unless I want to eat live snails or kelp.

I really, really don't.

As soon as the mermaids are done, Scylla has us line up in a semicircle in front of her. "It is time, at last," she says, her voice echoing straight into my head. "I am so tired. It is time for you to sing and for me to sleep." She narrows her eyes and looks at each of us in turn. "The doors are barred; you cannot escape while I slumber. Do not try, or I will be harsh with you."

I glance at Allora and Jasmina. They both look scared.

I don't know what Scylla would do if she didn't need us. Flick us away like she did Peter? Or take the breath gift away and watch me drown? That's what monsters do in stories—and gods, too. Maybe that's how you feel about people when you're immortal . . . that they're not important enough to worry about. When you're a monster and everyone who sees you wants to kill you.

"Land girl, you begin," Scylla says. "The others may join in with you. The song you were singing when I took you, about a lark."

I feel like I did when I was standing on the rock, worrying that she'd come. That I can't do this. But I have to.

I take a breath—without really taking a breath—and begin, singing over the dogs.

"Alouette, gentille alouette. Alouette, je te plumerai."

I do my best, pretending I'm performing in that choir I imagined. Right away two of the dogs, one on each side of her waist, go quiet, heads raised like they're listening. They look like normal dogs when they're not barking their heads off. Almost sweet. The others keep barking, and the eels writhe.

Nothing about this is sweet. I shudder, and my voice trembles, but I keep going.

"Je te plumerai la tête . . ."

163

The dogs start to close their eyes, their heads drooping. Allora and Jasmina join in with background harmony, since they don't know the words. And it works! The other four dogs stop barking. All you can hear is the sound of our voices intertwining, echoing in the cave. It's surprisingly beautiful.

The quiet is amazing, even to me, and I've only been around the dogs for a few hours. I can't imagine what it's like for Scylla.

She smiles and closes her eyes. I think she's asleep in seconds. Her face relaxes, and her mouth drops open. Her body falls back against the seat, the tentacles limp. One of the dogs moans, but it doesn't wake.

I finish the song, and for a moment there's complete quiet, and peace. Then the dogs start to rouse again, and I realize the truth.

We're going to have to keep singing. If we stop they'll wake up again, and so will she.

I was hoping we could escape once she fell asleep. At least try, in spite of her warning.

Jasmina quickly starts a new song, a mermaid song I don't understand, but now I do the background vocals. The dogs stay asleep, but only as long as all three of us are singing.

She's definitely not going to let us leave.

A tear slips down my face. I don't want to live my life in an underground cave singing for a monster. But I have no idea how I'm going to escape. I miss Fergus. And Mom. What if I can't ever see them again?

Allora reaches out and gently wipes the tear away, with a little shake of her head. I understand, without her saying a word. Crying is not going to help us. We can't think about how bad our situation is. We're all in this together, and we've got to be strong.

Maybe we can try to escape when she's in a deeper sleep. Maybe if the dogs sleep for a while, they won't wake up right away, and we can figure out how to break through the magic barrier, and swim to the surface, and . . .

For now, the dogs wake up every time we pause. We keep singing, on and on. For hours.

Fergus

Pixie and I run up the path toward the top of the mountain, as fast as we can in the dark. It feels like I'll be able to hear better up there.

If it's barking, it has to be Scylla. And Clover. Maybe I can see where they are.

Next to the waterfall, my heart starts to pound again, my head filling with pressure. It's too loud. Way too loud. The roaring sound crushes everything else out. I cover my ears like before, but it still doesn't help. And now I'm alone, except for Pixie, who moves to my shoulder. I don't know what to do to make it stop, to make it past the falls, but I know I have to keep going.

I sing the Lost Boys song under my breath, even though the waterfall smashes all the words.

> *Left, right, left*
> *We're off on an adventure*
> *Left, right, left*
> *We're going to fight a foe!*

That helps. Even without the Lost Boys here, I can almost feel them around me, laughing, singing.

I keep pushing on up the slope, watching my feet on the wet ground so I won't slip. The sound of the waterfall slides away behind me. My legs burn, but I think of Perseus and Odysseus—and Clover—being brave, and I keep going, up and up, Pixie with me. Now that the waterfall is behind us, I can hear the barking again, relentless.

Why can I hear it now, when we couldn't before? Is Scylla closer? It doesn't sound as loud as when she was at the surface. More that I can just hear it better. Maybe we were all just too loud, before. Maybe sound carries differently in the night.

It doesn't matter. I just need to know where it's coming from. It's a clue, I know it. Peter says Neverland always gives clues.

I come around the curve at the crest and stop. The view—the world—is magnificent from here. The sea stretches in all directions, still that black, moving mass, but it's the stars that make me go still. I've never seen so many stars, or even half so many stars. Every inch of the sky is filled with clusters and points of light. I can see the Milky Way, Andromeda, Cassiopeia, Pegasus. And Perseus! I've never seen Perseus in the sky before.

The barking gets quieter. I scan the ocean, to see if I can tell where it's coming from. Nothing. It gets quieter still. Then it drops off completely, and I want to cry. I didn't discover anything. It was the clue, and I missed it.

Except there's something else now, the sound whispering over the water. It's faint, but I recognize Clover's voice, and two other voices too, twisted together in a high melody. It's so quiet I lean over, toward the ocean, so I can listen better. The music soars up from the sea and around the stars.

My heart leaps, filling me with pure happiness and relief. Pixie flies around my head wildly. The music gets a little louder, like it's celebrating with us.

Clover really is alive. So are the other two mermaids. They're under the waves, but they're singing for Scylla like we thought, and they're *alive*.

And just like that, I know why. The dogs stopped

when Clover and the mermaids started singing. That's why Scylla wanted them. That's why she kept them. She *needs* them. They're singing the dogs to sleep for her. And if we know that, we can surely get them back.

I take out my recorder, hit the red button, and stand very, very still. I don't know that anyone will be able to hear the singing on the recorder, or understand what it is. But I want to try to capture that sound, all three of them singing together. I have an idea, and it's a place to start.

I don't know how long I stand there on the edge of the cliff, listening to Clover sing under the waves like a siren. Long enough for the sky to lighten at the rim of the sea, for the stars to begin to fade.

I give the water—and Clover—one last look, hit Stop, and head back down to the Lost Boys, trotting, Pixie resting on my shoulder. I feel so much better than when I left the house. I understand. I got the clue. And there's a way to save them, I know it.

I'm not a hero, even in Neverland. I'm still just Fergus. But I am going to get my sister back.

Clover

We try to escape when it's almost morning. First Jasmina slips off, singing still as she goes to the door, throwing her body against the opening. But she cries out with the pain of it, and stops singing, and the dogs stir, grumbling to themselves.

I go next, to look in the other room, Scylla's private room. It isn't even barred with magic. Still singing as loud as I can, I check every inch of it, looking for some sort of exit, or trigger, or anything. But there isn't any window or door, and the room is nearly empty. It has a chair like the one Scylla's sleeping in now, a table with containers of what looks like paint, some brushes like horsetails . . . and a pile of bones that look human. All covered with a net to keep them down on the table.

The dogs start to whine and I leave, shaking my head. I check the rest of the walls for secret panels, or anything, but there really is no way out.

Allora doesn't even try. She just keeps singing in her high, otherworldly voice, on and on and on. Jasmina and I join her again. We sing until we can't anymore, until our voices are hoarse and we're drooping, leaning against each other for support.

I think I'm the first to actually stop, my eyes so heavy I have to close them for just a second. It feels so nice, letting the heaviness pull me in. . . .

I snap awake to the sound of the dogs barking. Four of them, then all six start in, as loud as dogs can get.

Scylla's awake too, sitting up on the chair, staring at us.

I glance at Allora and Jasmina. They look as scared as I feel, shrinking back against the table. Ready to run away, even though we can't. We failed Scylla. We let the dogs wake up. How is she going to punish us?

She stretches her arms and smiles. "I slept!" She leaps up, swims to the ceiling of the cavern, then back down, zigzagging in the water like Fergus did in the air when he was flying. "I must have slept for *hours*. For the first time in hundreds . . . thousands of years. I slept! It worked!" She beams at us, the eels writhing madly. They were asleep too. She frowns, just a little. "You may sleep now. I will go out so you will have peace from the dogs."

Allora and Jasmina swim to the room they were in when I found them, so I follow. All I want to do is sleep, my body screaming to lie down somewhere. Ideally in my own bed, at home, with Fergus snoring peacefully across the room. Next best would be Grandmother and Grandfather's house, in the big nursery. Or even my bed with the Lost Boys.

This room is dark, with round stone walls, like Scylla's room. There are no openings except the door that's hung with seaweed. The room doesn't have any beds, of course. That wouldn't work under the ocean, with wet sheets. Instead there are three . . . nests. Round piles of soft leaves and plants, with some thick branches supporting them and holding everything together, like bird nests. The insides are lined with mounds of moss. It does look soft, at least.

"When did she make these?" I ask.

No one answers. Allora goes straight over to one and lies down, curled up in the bottom like a ball. She tugs a band of kelp from the side, pulls it over her waist, and pokes the end through a stick on the other side, like a seat belt.

I look at Jasmina, who laughs. "Otherwise you'd float right out of it. Here, get in. I'll fix you up."

I lie in the nest, and she pulls the strap of kelp over me, like a mother buckling a baby into a car seat. "Good rest," she whispers. "Happy thoughts."

It makes me miss Mom, even though she hasn't put me to bed for a long time. I smile drowsily at Jasmina. "Happy thoughts," I say.

It is surprisingly comfortable, once I snuggle in. I close my eyes. The last thing I hear is the dogs, fading away as Scylla leaves.

I wake to Allora poking me in the arm. It feels like I've only been asleep for a few minutes. "Go away," I murmur. "I'm not ready to get up." I squirm from the finger, back into sleep.

"Wake!" Allora whispers. "She did not bar our door, and she is still gone. We're going to try to escape."

I try to sit up, forgetting the seat belt, and fall back again. Without comment, Allora flicks the kelp off the stick and holds out a hand to pull me up. I don't take it, rubbing my eyes. I drift up slowly anyway.

"But what if we can't get out, and she finds out we tried?" I ask. I remember her saying "I ate men whole," and I shudder. I remember the panic of not being able to breathe. I remember the bones.

Allora shrugs her shoulders. "We must take that risk. It may be our only opportunity. Otherwise we could be trapped here for years." She stretches her hand out again. "Come, we must go."

I let her pull me away from the comfy nest. Jasmina is by the doorway, holding the kelp curtain open. "Hurry!" she says. "She could return at any moment."

I swim through the curtain, out into the large central room. I wonder why Scylla didn't bar the room. Did she forget? Was she so happy with her sleep that she thought we didn't need it? Or is it a test?

If it's a test, we're going to fail. But they're right: we have to try. If we can make it, and we swim all the way up to the island, I'm going to get as far inland as I can. I need to make sure she can't pull me down again. Though it's not as easy for the mermaids, of course. We'll need to figure that out once we're back up there.

But first we need to get out.

Allora swims to the front door but bounces right back, with a grimace. "She did not forget this one," she says.

We look at each other, not yet ready to give up and go back to our little room. I try it, reaching out my hand. The magic jolt is painful, like brushing your fingers on a hot stove. I cradle my hand. "What now?"

That's the only exit. We know that. The rest of this place is solid rock. Unless we can figure out a way to break the magic, we can't escape.

"What if we try it together?" Allora says quietly.

We look at each other. We have nothing to lose by trying. We link arms, and try to swim, sideways, through the door.

We bounce back, stung by the magic, separated. It doesn't work.

Jasmina lifts her head sharply. "Dogs."

Allora gasps. "She's coming. Back to the room, *now*."

I don't hear anything, but we go, as fast as we can. Through the curtain, back into the nests. I hear the dogs now, louder and louder. I forget the strap and start to float up just as I hear Scylla come in the house. She'll be in here any minute. I grab the sticks, yank myself down, and fling the strap across myself, stabbing the kelp over the stick and closing my eyes just in time.

The kelp curtain is yanked aside. My eyes are still scrunched tight, but I hear the dogs yelping, and feel Scylla's presence. It smells like wet dog.

I hold my breath as though I had breath to hold.

"My little songbirds have been out of their nests," she says quietly. None of us move. None of us breathe. How does she know? Did touching the magic signal her, like an alarm? "There is no escape from me. You will be here always. Always and forever. You should accept that."

There's a long pause, all of us silent.

"You will learn your lesson," she says at last. "And you will not try to leave me again." My heart thumps. Even though her voice is soft, there's a hard bitterness underneath. I know she means it. "Sleep well, my song-birds."

She pulls the kelp curtain closed, and it's utterly, utterly dark.

I think we just made everything worse.

26

Fergus

The Lost Boys think the recorder is magic.

I forgot they've never seen any technology before. No TVs, no cell phones, not even any radios. Ever. Peter said they don't have many visitors who don't show up as Lost Boys (or Girls). The last visitor was many years ago, when they fought the bear. Peter's probably seen some technology in people's houses when he goes to London—though he doesn't admit it—but none of the others have left this island since they came here.

What would that be like, to only know the lagoons and mountaintop and the house under the ground? To never watch a movie, or even read a book? Never go to school? I don't know if I feel sorry for them or envy them. Or both.

They huddle around me, whispering like I have a magic wand in my hand, when I haven't even done anything yet.

As soon as I got back down from the mountain, I woke them all up and told them what I had heard, what it meant, and what I thought we could do. It took a long time to get all the words out the right way so they understood—I was too excited, I think, and the words wouldn't come. But nobody seemed to mind. They don't look at me strangely when I take too long or the words are wrong or I can only make sounds. I love that.

First thing is to find out if we can hear the recording of the singing well enough.

I turn the volume all the way up. Then I go to the beginning of the file, press Play, and cross my fingers.

It's there. The sound of Clover and the two mermaids singing floats quietly through the air, sounding even more otherworldly from the machine. Well, it *is* coming from another world. Under the ocean.

The Lost Boys go absolutely silent, listening. I let it play for a long time, three or four whole songs, and nobody moves, like they're afraid to break the spell. Finally I hit Stop. Friendly touches me lightly on the arm.

"Beautiful," he says, his voice soft. I glance up and see Shoe's eyes filled with tears. Even Peter looks stunned, his eyebrows high.

"They are safe," he says. "That is most important. And this device will play again? Whenever you like?"

"Whenever you like," I echo. I nod. "Whenever you like."

In the distance, thunder booms. I look up, startled. Clouds are gathering, hiding the stars. I think it's going to rain.

"But the device cannot go under the water," Peter says.

"No," I say. "Submerging it in water would ruin the electronics. Especially seawater."

"How does it work?" Shoe asks. "It's so small. How can it hold the voices?"

I frown, trying to put my thoughts in order and think of the answer. "It's a digital recorder," I say. "So it records onto . . . a chip, I guess." They all stare blankly at me—they have no idea what a chip is—and I look down again at the recorder. "I don't know, really. But it doesn't matter. Can we get Scylla to hear it? It's not loud enough now. Can we make it loud enough?"

That's the question, and my whole plan. I want to amplify the sound so Scylla will be able to hear it, way down under the water. And then she'll come up to find out what it is, and how the singing could possibly be up here when she has Clover and the others down there. I don't think she's heard of a recorder either, even though she is a goddess. Then we can find a way to record them singing better, louder, and leave *that* for Scylla to listen to. I bet she doesn't need the singers in person to get the dogs to sleep. She just needs the songs. If we can figure out how to make her hear this, then we can figure out a way to play her a recording of it whenever she wants. Peter could play it every night from the island.

And she can let Clover go.

I like this plan, because it doesn't depend on me using a sword to chop Scylla's head off, like Peter was going to, or kill Medusa to turn Scylla to stone, like Perseus, but I can still save Clover. I just have to solve a puzzle, with help. A couple of puzzles. I like puzzles. And I have lots of help.

Thunder again, closer, and this time I see the lightning crack over the trees. Then thunder again. I smell ozone in the air.

Peter steps forward, his hands on his hips. "It's like making a trap. We've done lots of traps." He grins. "Lost Boys, remember when we laid a trap for the Bad Dragon?"

They all nod, and smile back. Though the Lost Boys don't seem to cheer as much, or as easily, since Peter was thrown into the sea and Clover was taken. Even the pixies seem to have less energy.

Peter lifts his chin. "We will do it. We can build on this plan of yours, Fergus. We will get them back, and defeat the monster that way."

The first drops of rain spatter onto the leaves. I carefully slip the voice recorder into my pocket, then hold out my hands and raise my face to the rain, letting it wash over me. My heart lifts a little. Neverland is made of magic, and I think it likes me. It let me hear the barking and the voices. It gave me Pixie to help with the cave and the bats. All the Lost Boys are here. I have help.

I have friends.

I think maybe we can do it. We can get them back.

My worry is, what if Scylla changes her mind, or loses her temper, before then? What if we're too late?

Clover

When I wake up again, it's still dark. Not even a little bit of light seeps through. I blink and yawn. I wonder what time it is. It feels like I slept for a year.

Then I remember what happened last night, Scylla catching us trying to escape, and I go cold. We're going to "learn our lesson" not to leave, she said. She's going to punish us somehow. I hear the dogs barking in the next room, so she's there, awake. I think I hear Allora and Jasmina breathing evenly, still sleeping.

My stomach growls loudly. I haven't eaten since the Feast on the beach.

I wish I could stay here in the nest as long as possible.

Scylla is scary. But that's not brave. What would Wendy do now?

I think she'd get up, get something to eat, and face Scylla for her punishment. Probably with her arms crossed, defiant.

I sigh. It's better than hiding. I fumble around for the kelp strap and manage to pull it off by feel. I struggle out of the nest and make my way, in the dark, to the door.

I pull the curtain open, but it's still dark. I frown, confused. Even in the middle of the night there was plenty of light in here, from the glowing paint.

"Good day," Scylla says in her low, scratchy voice.

I can't see her. I turn toward her voice, still standing with one hand on the curtain. "Hello."

"Having trouble, my little Demodocus?" she asks. Her voice turns nasty. "That will teach you to cross me. Singers have no need of sight."

I gasp as I realize the truth. It's not dark. I just can't see.

I'm blind.

My grip on the curtain tightens. Suddenly the rest of the world, the rest of this place, feels terrifying, unknown. How can I take a step forward, when I don't know what's there?

I feel the tears stream from my eyes, even though I

can't see. This is the punishment. And it's worse than I could have imagined.

"Why did you do this?" I ask. It sounds like a croak. "Why?"

Scylla doesn't answer.

I try to listen over the dogs, to hear what else might be going on. I can't hear anything except a slight clink, then another. I reach my hand out, but it's zapped back by the lock. I shake it out, from the pain. I stand there, helpless, gripping the kelp. Because I don't know what else to do.

The dogs bark in excitement, close, and I step back instinctively, my hands blocking my face.

"Come," she says, almost gently. "You must be faint from hunger. I found you food while you were trying to escape."

My stomach growls again in answer. But I don't move. I don't know which way to go.

"There is fruit, from the land by the shore. And humans eat clams still, yes?" Scylla asks. "I remember eating them, long ago."

"My mom does. I haven't." I swallow, thinking of Mom expertly popping clamshells open with a knife. "I don't know how." My voice shakes, wishing for Mom. For home. For Fergus. I rub my eyes, like that will make them work again.

I can't handle this. Not this on top of everything else.

I feel Scylla's hand in mine, tugging me out into the middle of the room. She pushes me down on a chair. I hang on to the sides.

"I shall open the clams for you, little land girl."

She hands me something, and I touch it all over. It's smooth, curved, with hard points on both ends. A banana. I manage to peel it and devour it in five bites.

I hear a scraping noise, then a pop. She takes the banana peel, opens my hand, and drops something into it like a present, something squishy and wet. Juice drips through my hand. I lift it to my nose. Clam. Fergus would never eat this—the texture is horrible. But I have seen Mom eat it at restaurants. And I'm so hungry.

I tip it into my mouth all at once, and chew. It tastes like ocean: salty, a little sweet. A little bit fishy.

Scylla laughs and hands me another. We don't say anything else until I've eaten four clams, another banana, and some melon.

"Better?" she asks.

I nod. Though I think of eating like this always, clams in the dark, and I want to cry again. I grip the chair so hard my fingers hurt.

"I was happy once," she says softly. "I had everything, but I did not know it. A family who loved me, and a good home. We lived in Greece, in the time when the gods were active in the world. My father was a god—I was a minor goddess—and I was beautiful, so I had attention from everyone. I thought it wonderful. I thought it would last forever."

One of the dogs growls and snaps. She sighs, loud. "In one moment, everything changed. After Circe's magic, I was a hideous beast, and the people drove me away. Even my parents wanted me gone. Even the man who made this happen. Glaucus." She spits the word. "He loved me for my beauty only, and when it was taken . . . he went away. I lived alone for so many years, rooted to the spot across from Charybdis, killing men. That was my whole life."

"Did you ask Circe to change you back?" I ask.

There's silence for a long moment, the question hanging in the air. I still hear the dogs barking and grunting, so I know she's there.

"No," she says at last. "That would be impossible."

I frown. "But why? If she made you like this, she could change you back. She's powerful enough. Wouldn't she listen?"

"You can't reason with a witch," Scylla snaps. "She only thinks of herself. She does not play fair."

I go very still. And then I take a risk.

"What you've done to me isn't fair," I whisper.

It's hard to know her reaction because I can't see, but I'm still sitting here, so I guess that's a good sign. I take another risk. "Maybe if you asked her, after all this time," I continue slowly, "she'd see that what she did was wrong, and change you back."

The sound of the barking is different, which I think means she's moving.

"You do not understand," she says from farther away. "Gods are merciless, always."

"But you're different than you used to be," I say. "You said you got tired of killing, and lived peacefully in your cave. Maybe she did too?"

There's another long pause. "I may be able to find where Circe is," she says.

I try not to get too hopeful. But if she's willing to go talk to Circe, and it works, maybe Scylla will give me my sight back. If Circe is merciful, maybe Scylla can be too.

And if Scylla were really changed back, she wouldn't need us anymore.

"She couldn't make it worse, could she?" I ask. "From what Fergus says, she was kind to Odysseus in the end."

"Who is this Fergus?" Scylla asks. "Is he a human or a god?"

I laugh. "He's my brother. He knows a lot about stories. He knew about you."

There's a pat on my hand and I feel, for the moment, like I've pleased her. Which is better than angering her again.

There's a sudden scream from the nest room, then another. Allora and Jasmina are awake. I think Scylla blinded them too.

Fergus

Shoe and I sit on the sand, hollowing out a watermelon with silver spoons. It's like hollowing out pumpkins on Halloween, except it's not as slimy, and there aren't gross strings like pumpkins have. I don't normally do that part anyway. I don't like the smell, or the slime on my fingers, so Mom does it for me. I carve it, though. Last year I carved one that looked like Thor's hammer. Clover did hers at her friend's house. It was the first time she didn't carve it with us.

I was mad she wasn't there. But it's different if she's gone because she's happy somewhere else. Mom said that. Now she's gone because she was stolen.

I drop another spoonful of watermelon onto the sand. This has to work. I don't have another idea if it doesn't. The other Lost Boys are off looking for another melon, if we mess this one up. Peter is with the mermaids getting conch shells.

It has to work.

"What is your home like?" Shoe asks.

I frown. The question triggers a rush of memories of home: smells, sounds, textures. Mom and Clover. Comfort. Familiar. But I wouldn't know how to organize any of that into something I could say.

I don't answer.

Shoe doesn't seem to mind. "Do you live in London?" she asks. "Peter tells us stories about London. The big clock Ben, and the river with ships, and all the houses with lights glowing in the windows."

I shake my head. "Our grandparents live in London. We live in San Diego. In California." I think how to describe it. "It's by the ocean, and sunny most of the time. There are seals and sea lions and cliffs."

Shoe sits back on her heels, looking out at the waves. "Cal-i-for-nia," she repeats in her Neverland-British accent. "I like the sound of London better." She sighs. "A city, with people and bustle and fun. Adventures everywhere. I only remember living by the ocean. Here." She starts scooping again, leaning over the watermelon. Her hair hangs across her face. "But I think I might have been from London . . . before. I don't know why. It's not quite a memory. I just . . . feel it."

I haven't really thought of where the Lost Boys came from. Or why. Did they really get lost? Or did they just not fit in with their families? Or did their families die, and they had nowhere else to go?

"You should go to London with Peter sometime," I say. "It's not that far."

She doesn't answer. She looks out at the ocean again, at Peter up to his ankles in the surf talking to the mermaids, then sighs and goes back to the job. We scoop melon until the inside is clean, but not all the way to the white rind. Then Shoe sets the lid back on, making sure the fit is tight. Peter tromps back up the beach with two perfect conch shells. He stands above us, the shells drip-dripping on the sand.

"Are you ready?" he asks. "I want to have a go at this monster again."

I look up at him, eyebrows high. That's not what we're doing. "We're just talking to her," I say.

He shrugs, and the tips of his ears go pink. "I have never lost," he says. "I do not like the feeling."

When I look back, Shoe has cut the slot for the

recorder. It's precise, exactly the right size. "We will have to hold it in here," she says. She looks up at Peter. "I can come with you and hold it."

Peter frowns at her, then nods. "I will call the rest of the Lost Boys, we will test this machine, and then we will meet the monster again. We shall not be defeated this time." He touches the sword sheathed again at his back, and nods.

Anxiety claws at my chest. I hope Scylla listens . . . but I hope Peter does too. I don't want him taking over the plan and attacking Scylla again.

But Peter Pan does what he wants to do. I don't think I could stop him.

Peter and Shoe and I stand on the flat rock in the middle of the lagoon, with the voice recorder and the amplifier.

It looks like something you might make for a science fair.

Shoe holds the recorder in the slot in the hollowed-out watermelon. At either end we attached the two conch shells, pointing out. The sound goes down into the melon and out through the shells, and comes out much louder.

It's a fancy speaker made of fruit and shells.

It looks funny, but it works. I think it might win if it

were in the science fair. We tested it on another sound file, one I made of the ocean. It was almost as loud as the waterfall.

And now we're ready. One of the mermaids carried the amplifier above her head across the lagoon, and Shoe and I swam out with Peter. I held the recorder high so it wouldn't get wet. I'm a good swimmer. Mom had us both take lessons at the Y.

I look at Peter, and he looks at me. He grins.

I don't grin. Scylla might steal us away, or do something else terrible. But this is for Clover. This is our plan. I take a deep breath.

"Ready," I say.

Shoe presses Play.

The sound of Clover and the mermaids singing bursts into the air, so loud I flinch.

We wait, letting the song sink into the air and the water. It's really not long before the water starts to twist below us. I don't hear dogs, but then I shouldn't, if that's what the song is for. "It's working," I whisper.

"Be ready," Peter answers. He touches the sword again. He doesn't draw it, but he looks eager to fight, his fists clenched on his hips. His freckles are darker than usual. *Don't fight, Peter,* I think. *That would ruin everything.*

Shoe clenches her jaw. She actually *looks* brave.

Scylla erupts out of the water, eels snapping around her head, but the dogs are quiet, drowsy. I duck, like Clover did. But Scylla doesn't throw me or Peter off the rock. She looks down at us, and at the speaker, confused. "What is this magic?" she booms.

I reach down, pull the recorder out, and show it to her. I hit the Stop button, and the sound cuts off. Instantly the dogs open their eyes and start barking again. Scylla's face creases.

I need to explain, but all the words have flown out of my mind. What was I supposed to say? What are the words? I can't think. I can only watch the eels and the dogs.

Focus, focus. I tap my fingers together and look at them instead. Tap, tap, tap. I know the rhythm, the feel of it, so well. It settles my mind.

I talk, but I keep looking at my hand, not at her.

"It's a voice recorder," I say. "It can capture sounds and replay them whenever you want." Tap, tap, tap. Focus. "I recorded the singing so you could put the dogs to sleep anytime. It has to stay on land, but someone on the island could play it for you. You can let my sister and the mermaids go."

Scylla doesn't say anything for a long time, just stares down at me while I focus on my fingers. Finally I look up, at her eels and her face.

"Your sister," she says. "You are Fergus?"

I blink. "Yes."

"You know stories about gods and goddesses," she says. "You knew about me."

"Yes," I answer again, puzzled.

"What do you know of Circe, Fergus?"

"Be careful," Peter warns, shifting behind me.

Scylla glances at him, then at Shoe, like she's just noticed them. Like a mountain lion noticing prey.

I don't know what exactly to be careful of, but she asked something I know the answer to. "Circe was the goddess who transformed you," I say. "Because Glaucus loved you and she was jealous. She transformed men into beasts, using the herb mandrake. She transformed Odysseus's men into pigs. But Odysseus was warned, by Hermes, to eat a different herb before he met her that would make him impervious to her magic. He did, and he was safe. She fell in love with him, too."

Scylla lowers herself down in the water, inch by inch, until her giant face is even with mine. I look down at my fingers again.

"And what is this herb he ate, land boy?"

This close, she smells like fish.

Peter takes a step closer to me. I feel him at my back. I'm not sure it makes me any calmer.

"Moly," I whisper. "They think it's a snowdrop." I

195

close my eyes and quote from Homer. "'The root was black, while the flower was as white as milk; the gods call it moly.' It has white flowers that look like they're drooping."

"I know where that is!" Shoe says.

Scylla flicks her gaze to Shoe.

"I saw that once in the forest," she says, low. She glances at Peter. "By Pixie Hollow."

I stare at the eels writhing around Scylla's head. I try to think of what color she is, but she doesn't seem to be a color. Maybe just gray, like waves on a cloudy day.

"Pan," she snaps. "This is your land—you must be aware of the other gods. Circe fled to an island like this one. Do you know where she has her home?"

I draw a sharp breath. Scylla called him Pan. And a god.

Peter flushes. "I have heard . . . it is not far," he chokes. "I do not go there. None go there."

Suddenly Scylla lays a hand on mine. I think she's trying to stop me from tapping—to keep my hands quiet—but I feel something else happen, some change sweep across my body that I can't identify.

"I have given you the breath gift, Fergus," she says softly.

"The breath gift?" I ask.

"To breathe underwater. You"—she points at Shoe—"will go and gather this moly for us. Pan will tell me exactly where to find Circe. And you, Fergus, will come with me back to my house, to your sister. I will let you both go when Circe returns me to my former self."

Peter leans close to my ear. "It's a god's bargain," he whispers urgently. "You know how gods' bargains are. Mortals never do well."

He's right. In all the myths, mortals come to a bad end whenever they go with gods . . . or monsters.

"I can do that," Shoe says.

I'm afraid: to go underwater, to be so out of control, so unknown. But if it will save Clover, it's what we have to do. I don't think I have any other choice.

"Yes," I say.

Peter stands tall, hands on his hips. "I will go with you, not Fergus. He can identify the herb, so he will go with Shoe. And I must see that the mermaids are all right, that Clover is all right. As you said, this is my land. My responsibility."

I suck in a breath. I don't have to go underwater?

Scylla narrows her eyes. "Very well. You may take the boy's place, for now."

Peter turns back to me. "Keep the recorder safe," he whispers. "We may still need it to get your sister back."

"You will meet me here with the herb when the sun is high," Scylla says. She looks at me—to make sure I understand, I think—and I nod. Then she tugs Peter's hand, and he slips off the rock and slides down, down, down into the water.

Shoe and I watch him go, then swim as fast as we can for the shore. I hold the recorder out of the water again. I'll give it to Friendly to keep, and then we'll find the moly. We only have an hour or so until the sun is high.

We have to hurry.

29

Clover

The three of us sit in the main room, unmoving. Scylla's punishment has worked—even though she's gone up to the surface to see where the singing came from, we don't dare try to go anywhere. I wouldn't even know which way was up, in the open ocean.

Maybe someday I'll be brave enough to try, sight or not, but for now being blind has grounded all of us firmly in our chairs, waiting.

I squeeze my fingers tight around the chair arms. That singing had to come from Fergus. I hope he stays far, far away from Scylla.

Before long I hear the dogs barking again, and Scylla

bursts back through the doorway. Then there's another rush of sound behind her.

"Clover?" a familiar voice says. "Allora, Jasmina? Are you all right?"

"Peter?" I ask, straining to see. Why is he here?

"I almost forgot," Scylla says.

There's a snap, and suddenly I can see again, as clear as ever. Clearer, maybe. Peter's face is sharp, concerned.

I jump up and hug him. He staggers a little, surprised, but hugs back. He must have done something. He must have convinced Scylla to release us.

But I look back at the table, and Jasmina and Allora haven't moved. They still can't see. "Peter?" Jasmina asks. "Have you come to save us?" Tears fall from her cheeks. "Please, let us go. Let us see."

"Please!" Allora stretches out her hands.

"Enough!" Scylla snaps. "The mermaids are here and alive, Pan, as you witness. I will keep them here for now. I do not trust this device of yours. It may be another trick."

"It is not a trick!" Peter says. "And I will go on this adventure with you. You have no need to keep them any longer."

Wait, what adventure?

"Please," Jasmina says again.

"Mermaids, to your room!" Scylla explodes out of

her chair, towering over all of us. The dogs burst into a frenzy of barking and howling. "I will not argue this!"

We're all silent. Jasmina and Allora swim to their room, and Scylla sets the boundary at the door.

"Are you truly all right?" Peter whispers.

"I am now. She's powerful, though. She took our sight," I whisper back. I look at him closely, because I can. His red curls float all the way around his head. His eyes are even greener in the water. He looks . . . softer than he did up above. Less sure of himself. He has his sword again, sheathed at his back. I'm surprised Scylla didn't object, but I guess he can't hurt her easily. "Be careful of her," I say.

"I can hear you," Scylla says behind us. "But thanks to Pan and your brother, and your idea, I have other plans for you now."

Plans? That sounds bad. My idea?

"Oh! You're going to face Circe?" I ask.

"*We* are." There's hope in Scylla's voice, for the first time. "To ask for my life back. I had not thought . . ." She touches one of the shell sculptures on the wall, the one of the spreading tree. "Pan knows where she is," she says softly. "Your brother and the other land girl are fetching the herb, to protect you from her magic. We will meet them. And we will all go, together."

I stare at her. "We will *all* go?" I ask, my voice a

squeak. "To face the witch-goddess who turns everyone into beasts? I thought . . . I thought you'd go by yourself."

"I said I would go," Peter adds. "Why the others?"

"My brother's not going," I say, as firmly as I can say it.

Scylla crosses her arms, and I can see her anger rising. The eels writhe; the dogs twist and snap.

I swallow hard. "He can't go," I say. "Okay, I'll go. Peter can go. . . ." I wave toward him. I feel like I'm giving him up, but then, he's Peter Pan. He can take care of himself. His expression doesn't change. "Shoe and Fergus can stay on the island, safe."

"I agree," Peter says.

Scylla comes closer still. "Are you not enamored of your sight, then?" she asks, so quiet I can barely hear her. "You would rather defy me and be blind? Or have your brother be blind? I can do that from here." She raises her arm.

"No!" I yell. I want to dive at her, to make her stop. Peter holds me back, his grip strong.

She stays like that, one hand high, for a few breaths, then slowly lowers it. "No," she echoes. "Your protectiveness is admirable. But your brother has knowledge of Circe, and the other land girl has knowledge of herbs.

Pan knows where she has her lair. You . . ." She studies me for a moment, her head tilted. "It was your idea. Now rest, calm yourselves, and prepare. We meet the others soon, and then we will be on our way."

She disappears into her back room.

"I'm sorry," I say to Peter, my voice wobbling. "I can't believe you're all dragged into this now."

I think I see fear in his eyes, for just a second. Then he raises his chin. "Do not be silly. This is an adventure, like all the others. It is just away from Neverland."

I sit on one of the chairs, staring up at the mural on the ceiling. Why do I keep messing up here? Why do I keep making everything worse, instead of protecting Fergus like I'm supposed to?

I don't have an answer. But it's true. I've just made everything so much worse.

Fergus

I try to think of everything I know about Circe.

Shoe is ahead of me on the path, chattering about something, but I'm not listening at all. I'm trying to re-member all the details. I wish I had my books with me, but I left them in the Lost Boys' house, in my backpack. I should've brought it everywhere, like Clover said.

Think. Circe was the daughter of Helios, the god of the sun, and Perse, an Oceanid. She had two brothers, Aeëtes and Perses, and a sister, P-something . . . I can't remember the sister's name.

Another book says her parents were Aeëtes and Hecate, I think.

She lived on the hidden island of Aeaea, which was somewhere near Italy, not far from Rome. But she doesn't live there now. Peter said she lives not far from here, wherever Neverland is. Maybe on another hidden island?

Scylla called him Pan, and said he'd know where the "other gods" were. Does that mean I was right? That he's *the* Pan, son of Hermes? That he's a god?

Are there gods hiding all over the world, pretending to be regular people? Or hiding away trying to avoid people? That's exciting. I wonder how many I could find.

We pass an orchard, and I briefly want to go in, to pluck the little red apples from the trees. They look so bright, so shiny, like Snow White's apple. But I can't. We have to get the herb, and get back to the rock. And see Clover.

"Fergus?" Shoe says.

I look up, away from the apples, and realize I stopped in the middle of the path.

Shoe smiles. "It's not much farther."

"Are you scared?" I ask.

She blinks, and the smile drops away. "Scared?"

"Of all of this. Facing Scylla again. What if she takes Clover with her, to see Circe? What if she takes us?"

Shoe looks at her feet, her hair covering her face again. "I would go with her," she says, super quiet. "I've never been away from Neverland. The really big adventures always happen to other people." She looks up, her eyes bright. "Anyway, isn't that what the moly is for, so humans can see Circe and she can't turn anyone into animals? We'd be safe." She turns and keeps going, and I follow. She's right: that is what the moly is for. If it's the right herb, if the legend is accurate, if it works. If the plant we find is really the right one.

Scylla is planning on taking mortals with her. That's the only reason she'd need it.

We take the path around to Pixie Hollow, where we found Shoe and Clover before, and go a little bit farther, to a forest just past it. I keep a close eye out for pixies, but I haven't seen any. I bet they're upset with Peter gone.

Shoe hunts around a little in the trees, and then makes a crowing noise and kneels down.

I see it: a snowdrop, just like the pictures. There are a few. Shoe looks at me to make sure she's right, and I nod. She plucks them, all the ones she can find, and puts them in a bag she has tied around her waist.

I like her. She thinks of things. She's like Clover. But different, too.

I feel something warm by my cheek, and then see it, the flutter of brightness. A pixie.

Shoe raises her arms, protecting her face. "We mean no harm! Peter sent us!" Her voice is higher than usual. "We need the snowdrop to counteract Circe's spells. It's to protect Peter, too."

The pixie flies around her in a circle, then zips off into the pixie village of houses. Shoe breathes a sigh of relief. "Let's get to the beach," she says. "Quick."

But a minute later, when we've barely taken a few steps, the pixie returns, with another pixie. They fly right past us, into the trees on the other side of the path . . . then come back and fly around my head.

I have the urge to bat them away. I stay very still so I won't. "We're going," I say. "Don't worry."

The pixies fly back into the trees, in the same spot as before, and then to me again, then to Shoe. Then back to the trees.

"Follow?" I ask.

One of the pixies bobs excitedly in front of my face.

Shoe laughs. "I guess they want us to follow them."

We follow, a ways into the trees. Then both pixies dart to the ground, to a little plant with clusters of round leaves next to an oak tree. One pixie flies to Shoe's bag, then to the plant again.

"Do we need this plant too?" Shoe asks.

The two pixies dance in the air, doing flips and flutters. I make my hands fly, imitating them. Shoe pulls up several handfuls of the plant, adding it to her bag.

"Thank you," I say.

One of the pixies flies close to my face, and I feel a brush of warmth. Then they fly off, back to Pixie Hollow.

Shoe ties the bag securely around her waist again. She looks at the sun, then raises her eyebrows at me. "Race you back?"

I smile. I do like Shoe.

31

Clover

I tread water behind Scylla, waiting. The sun is warm, and almost straight up in the sky. Peter's next to me.

We're by the flat rock where she took me. The land is so close, right there. If I could swim fast enough to the shore, scramble up onto the sand, maybe Scylla couldn't reach me. Then I wouldn't have to go find Circe. Fergus and Shoe wouldn't have to go. Peter could make it to shore, I'm sure. We'd be safe.

Except I can't swim that fast. And Scylla can blind us from anywhere—she said that. I don't know if it's true, but I don't want to find out.

Plus, Jasmina and Allora are still down there, in the

cave. Scylla wouldn't give them their sight back, wouldn't let them out. She said they had to stay in the cave until we came back. If Circe changes her, they're free. If not, maybe she'll try the recorder . . . or maybe she'll keep us after all.

It's not good to get on the wrong side of gods.

The mermaids are all at the other end of the lagoon now, watching from as far as they can get. The Lost Boys are in a little group at the top of the sand.

I guess we really don't have a choice now. We have to go, and do what Scylla wants. We're stuck.

Fergus too. I can't protect him at all.

"Do you really know where Circe is?" I ask Peter in a low whisper.

He swipes his wet hair off his face, looking uncomfortable. "I do."

"But you've never met her before?"

He shakes his head, his eyes clouded. "She is not someone you want to meet."

That doesn't make me feel better. I want cheerful, confident Peter, who says he can do anything. I go silent, watching the shore. I think I see them, far up the path. Something moving fast.

I don't want them to come. If Fergus would stay there, if he didn't come down here at all, maybe Scylla would give up the idea of bringing him, and he'd be okay . . . safe.

I definitely see them now, running hard. Shoe's hair is wild, her face serious.

Fergus looks worried. They run to the cluster of Lost Boys, huddle for a few minutes, and then head for the shore. I tread water, Peter next to me. It feels like we should be doing something.

Fergus and Shoe swim out, fast, and pull up, dripping, onto the rock.

Scylla actually smiles. She seems different. Lighter. A little more friendly than frightening, as if that splash of hope has changed her. I guess she hasn't had hope for a long time. "You have the herb?"

Shoe nods, eager. "And another one too. The pixies showed us." She takes a little plant with round leaves out of a bag, dripping wet. "I think you're supposed to eat them together. I don't know for sure, but I thought it would be a good idea to bring it, since they wanted us to."

Scylla looks at it. "That one will likely stop the moly from making you violently ill." She shrugs. "Helpful, I suppose."

No one answers. It would've been good to know it was going to make us sick.

Fergus looks right at me, his eyes wet. "Clover? You're okay?"

I feel the surge of matching tears in my chest, my throat. I push them down. "I'm okay. Are you?"

He doesn't answer, just stares at his hands, tapping. He looks okay.

"You two are coming with us also," Scylla says. "I may need your help." By her voice, it's clear that it's a demand, not a choice.

Fergus goes pale. But he looks at me and at Peter and swallows hard. "Okay."

Shoe blows out a long breath; then she nods. "I thought so."

"Come," Scylla says. She takes one of Shoe's hands, and one of Fergus's, and pulls them into the water. We don't even wave goodbye to the mermaids or the Lost Boys or the pixies. We just swim away.

Scylla's a fast swimmer.

I mean, of course she is—she's been in the water for thousands of years. She's a sea creature. She has tentacles. But I didn't really think about that until I had to try to swim with her.

She's holding on to Fergus and Shoe. Peter leads the

way. He's a strong swimmer too, even with a sword at his back.

I'm behind everyone else, just trying to keep up, trying to keep out of the way of Scylla's lashing tentacles. I don't have to breathe, but I still have to push my way through the water, without magic to help.

I wonder if Wendy could swim. I'm not sure. Did ladies swim back then? Would she have even been able to follow Scylla?

I bet she would. I really wish I could've met her.

They're getting ahead of me again. I work harder, pushing forward. I hope this island really isn't too far away.

We swim, and swim, and swim.

We come up to the surface after a while, for Peter to get his bearings. Scylla lets us sit on a craggy rock that's poking up alone out of the ocean.

I look around us for signs of other islands, for anything that will give me a clue where we are.

"Aren't the gods in Greece?" Shoe asks. Her wet hair drips in a solid sheet down her back. It makes her look a little bit like a mermaid. "All the stories Fergus told us were in Greece."

Scylla turns from scanning the horizon and raises her eyebrows. "Oh, not any longer. Greece and Italy are far too crowded with humans now, humans who do not believe in us, or have no knowledge of us. Most of us went far to the north, or far to the south, to the lands of ice." She shivers. "It is not what we were made for, but few humans find us now. We're hidden, in plain sight."

Fergus laughs, loud. When I look at him, he smiles. "I was right," he says. "They still exist. They are everywhere."

"You like this," I say, almost accusing.

He frowns, water trickling down his face. "Yes. It's an adventure. With gods and goddesses. It's what I wanted."

It's not what I wanted.

Peter and Scylla are talking again, pointing far off in the distance. I can't see anything they're pointing at.

"I like it too," Shoe says quietly. "It's a good adventure."

I frown and stare out at the ocean, my chin on my knees. "But aren't you afraid? Don't you want to go back? Home?"

Fergus considers, for a long time. "I miss Mom," he says finally.

I miss Mom too. I want to be with her. I want a giant, squeezy hug so much I can almost feel it. But I also miss so much more than Mom. Home, school, friends, the bustle of San Diego. A normal, regular schedule. The comfort of knowing there's someone I can go to for help if I want.

Fergus seems different too, since we came to Neverland. Here he's the strong one, the one who takes things in stride and handles them. I just mess up and make mistakes.

It's like he belongs here, in Neverland, and I belong at home.

Does he think that too?

"We are on course," Scylla says, the dogs barking excitedly. "It is close. Let us continue."

I sigh. We slide back into the water, which feels warmer now than the air, and keep swimming, and swimming, and swimming.

Fergus

Finally Peter gestures, and Scylla slows, then pulls us to the surface.

We've arrived at a little island shaped like a tall hat. The sides are giant, steep cliffs with birds screaming around them; then above that is a short, sloping hill, bright green, then a flat part. I don't see any houses or beach—or anything but cliff. We bob in the water, looking up.

"Where are we?" Clover asks.

"Top Hat," Peter answers. He shrugs. "That's what I call it. I have been told that Circe hides here—that it is hers. I told all the Lost Boys that it was surrounded by crocodiles, so they wouldn't go near it . . . if any ever came this far."

Shoe shudders, and I wonder what other stories Peter told them.

I just thought of something. "But how will you go see her?" I ask Scylla. "Can you walk on land?"

"Why do you think I brought you all, land boy?" Scylla snaps. "You will go find her, give her my message, and bring her to speak with me." She takes our hands and starts swimming again, steering us around the island. Clover and Peter follow. On the other side there's a massive pile of rocks. Dangling from the cliff above them is a rope ladder. "There. I knew there must be a way. Circe likes her supplicants. You will climb up and speak with her, and ask her to come down. Do not forget to chew your plants before you see her. She is used to finding clever ways to poison people."

Shoe nods and holds her bag up. No, we won't forget that. Scylla sets Shoe and me down on a slippery rock, and Clover and Peter scramble to shore. Clover looks pale in this light, and her hands are trembling. She stares up the cliff, up the scary rope ladder, and bites her lip. She doesn't like high things.

"I don't see how," she says. "We'll fall off."

Peter hops over to it and looks up, hands on his hips.

"Easy!" he says. Shoe follows, but she doesn't say anything. She doesn't look as certain.

I slip and slide across the rocks, using my hands to hold on some of the time, and grab hold of the ladder. It's rough, but like the climbing rope at the Autism Center, not so rough that it'll tear your hands. I'm good at climbing at the center. This is different, though. There's no mat underneath, or anyone to steady your feet. If you fall, there are just sharp rocks.

I look back at Scylla, looming half out of the water with her arms folded across her chest, the dogs yapping at us. "Can you protect us if we fall?" I ask.

She shakes the eels. "My magic has no sway here. This is Circe's domain."

"We do not need magic. I'll go first," Peter says. He grins, and I get a surge of faith. Maybe we can do this. "See you at the top."

I hold one side of the ladder, and Shoe holds the other, to keep it steady. Peter grabs hold confidently, steps on, and starts up, and up and up. I get dizzy when I lean back to look at him. There are seagulls at the top, flying in lazy circles. They cry every once in a while, disturbed by Peter.

I echo the sound back, quietly.

When Peter's about halfway, Shoe clears her throat.

"I will go next, if that is all right. At the top we can chew the plants before we go farther."

Clover nods, her arms crossed tightly. But she comes over and holds the other side of the ladder while Shoe starts up. Shoe doesn't climb as easily as Peter, but she still does well. She takes one rung at a time, her head always up, looking at the next one. That's the way to do it, I think. You can't ever look down.

When Shoe is halfway I look up, tilting my head far back, then at Clover. "You don't have to go," I say. "You don't like climbing. There are enough of us up there. You can hold the ladder for me, and stay here. And hold the ladder for us when we come down."

"Really?" I can't tell what she's thinking from her face. Too many emotions there, all mixed. But she always gets shaky when she's up high, and I know she doesn't want to go. Like she didn't really want to go to Neverland. "Are you sure?" she asks.

"Sure," I say. "My turn." I'm not certain I can make it. It looks terrifying. But it's our adventure, what we're here for. Peter went. Shoe went.

I take a deep breath and put my foot on the first rung of the ladder.

Suddenly Clover's arms are around me, hugging. I flinch, surprised. I don't really like it, but I know she means love. I squeeze back, sharing the love. We only do it for a second or two, then let go. Her eyes are full of tears. "Be careful," she says. "Don't fall, and don't let her trick you."

I nod, ready to start now before I lose my courage. "Don't let her trick you," I repeat.

Clover laughs a strange, hiccupy laugh and steps out of the way, one hand on the ladder again, pulling it steady. I lift my head, look up at the top one more time, and put one foot on, then the other. It's time to just climb.

Clover

I grip the rope as hard as I can, watching as Fergus climbs.

I didn't want to let him go without me. It feels wrong. But honestly, I've messed up everything I've touched here. I'm sure I'd just mess this up too: fall, or say something wrong to Circe, or put him and Shoe and Peter in more danger. It's probably better if I stay here.

He's climbing well. I'm fiercely proud of him. He didn't hesitate at all, just started doing what had to be done. The dog barking quiets, and I look back. Scylla has gone under the water again. She's not even going to watch. It's just me down here, alone at the bottom of the cliff.

Fergus is definitely different here. He's braver and stronger. I always knew he was smart, even when other people told him he wasn't. But I didn't know he was brave. He didn't really have the chance to be. I hate to think it, but was Grandfather right? Do I smother Fergus? Have I been keeping him from being brave—being his true self—this whole time, by not letting him try?

My eyes are so blurry that I can't see. I blink away the tears and check: he's about three-quarters of the way up. I pull tight on the rope, hanging my weight on it to keep it steady. Maybe that's why I've been having so much trouble in Neverland, on this adventure. Because I'm still too worried about Fergus and how he'll do, and not just letting myself *be* in Neverland. Be myself.

I'll be different when we get back home. I won't smother him and try to protect him from everything. I'll try to just let him be.

If we ever get back home. I look up at Fergus's feet, making steady progress. Fergus is about to face a legendary witch. To ask her to help a legendary sea monster. And even if everything works out okay, we're going back to Neverland after that. I honestly don't know if Fergus ever wants to go back home. I hold on to the ladder, staring out at the ocean, until suddenly it slackens. I squint all the way up and see Fergus's feet disappear over the top of the cliff.

He made it. He proved that he could do it.

I stand there, the gulls calling above me, looking out at the ocean. It looks so empty. I feel so, so alone.

I feel like a coward.

What am I doing down here? Why didn't I go up the cliff with the rest of them? Why did I stay here, safe?

"I can see we need to teach you about the Neverland," Peter said, that first night. "If you go to the Neverland, you go for fun. Adventure. Freedom."

Suddenly I know I have to go too. Not because I need to protect Fergus—he'll do fine without me— but because I don't want to be the sort of person who doesn't go, who stands at the bottom of a cliff and waits without even trying. Wendy would go. Mom would go, I think. Shoe and Peter and Fergus went already.

Fergus is brave. I can be too.

I put one foot on the ladder, and it sways. There's no one left to hold it for me. But that's okay. I can do this. I look up again at the terrible cliff, then decide I'm not going to look up anymore. I'm just going to look at the ladder, and keep going. I put the other foot on, grip the rope hard with both hands, and go.

It's much harder than they made it look. I have to use a lot of strength to pull myself up, and balance to set my feet in the right places. The cliff is right in front of my nose, bright white. It smells like bird droppings.

I stare at the folds and crevices as I go. Left arm up, left foot up, pull, right arm up, right foot. Keep moving. I get into a rhythm. Left, left, right, right. My arms are shaking, they're so tired. I stop, probably halfway, to rest. And then I look down.

The fear grabs at me, and I nearly fall. It's so far. It's so uncertain. I can't do it. I *can't*.

But I have to. I take a deep breath and keep going, one foot, one arm at a time, swaying, on and on. On and on and on, until the cliff edge appears above my head, green with grass, and I manage to pull myself up and over. I lie there for a minute in the grass, staring up at the sky, breathing hard. My arms and legs burn with effort. I didn't think I could do it, not really. But I made it.

That's only the first step, though. Now I have to catch up with the others, and find Circe. I roll over and push to my knees, and look around for the first time.

It's bare on the top: no trees, no bushes. Just a short stretch of grass, in a gentle slope. I can't see anything else. I get up, and force my wobbly legs up the slope. Once I'm on the flat top, I see one stone house in the far distance, surrounded by wisps of fog, with Fergus, Shoe, and Peter about halfway there. There are also sheep. A long-haired puff of a sheep with a black face is only a few steps away from me. It bleats, then runs off to join a crowd of them, all with ridiculously fluffy wool and black legs, staring hard at me.

Circe has sheep. That makes sense, if you live here alone. You can milk sheep and use the wool and meat. I hope they're real sheep and not the previous visitors to the island.

Then I remember—I didn't chew the plants. If Circe decides to turn me into something—a sheep, or a pig, or a monster like Scylla—there's nothing to stop her. The worst thing, in all the stories, is when you get magic help, like the plants, and don't use it properly. Then you're toast.

I have to go anyway. I'm here, and I didn't climb all that way for nothing, and the rest of them are already nearly there. The sun is shining full now, in my face, but I shade my eyes. Their shapes vanish into the mist. I have to go *now*, or it might be too late.

I run, the sheep bleating after me.

Fergus

It smells like sheep up here—musky, like a petting zoo—but also like something else, like lightning, hot and electric. Like magic. The air is full of it, almost visible. Peter said Circe was "hiding" here, but I think anyone who made it up the rope ladder would feel *something* was wrong, even if they didn't know what it was. The house sitting at the other end of the cliff even has mist curling around it, like in a movie.

Peter barely waited for me to get to the top, to recover my breath, before heading to the house.

Shoe did wait. She was doing cartwheels when I came up, but she stopped, hands on her hips like Peter, and gave me the two plants to chew, part of a white petal and stem and a handful of the leaves of the other one. I hesitate about the plants—I don't like foods that get all in my teeth—but I take them and put them in my mouth. When I chew, it tastes a little like lemon, and a lot bitter.

Shoe looks at the cliff edge, then frowns. "No Clover?"

I shake my head. "Waiting at the bottom."

Shoe sighs. "She is afraid. The fear gets all tangled in her head, and she can't go on."

I nod. It is exactly like that sometimes, though I haven't thought of it that way before. She always gets tangled about high places. I know the feeling of getting tangled.

We walk fast to catch up to Peter. I try to think of what to say to Circe.

I chewed the plants, so she can't poison me at least. But I'm still scared. Circe is all-powerful. Everyone was always afraid of her in the stories.

"Hi, I'm Fergus. Scylla sent me . . . ," I whisper. No. I don't want to tell her my name. Names have power with witches. "Scylla sent me. She's down below, in the water, and would like to speak with you."

That's not bad. It's strong and doesn't say anything

unnecessary. We're close to the house now, the mist reaching out for us. "Scylla sent me," I murmur. "She's down below, and would like to speak with you." I step into the mist. It curls around my head, and I breathe it in, wet. The little house is made of round stones, but the door is painted bright, forest green. Almost Peter's green.

Peter is already there, fidgeting. "Let's begin this," he says. He touches the sword at his back to make sure it's there. Then he knocks on the door twice.

I wasn't ready. "Scylla sent me," I rehearse quickly. Shoe grabs my hand—hers is sweaty and warm—and I let her for a second, then let go.

No one answers. Peter looks at me, shrugs, then knocks again. The door jerks open. At the same time Clover yells "Fergus!" behind us. I turn, surprised, and see her running, stumbling toward us. "Wait for me," she calls. But as soon as she reaches the mist—a second after she breathes it in—she vanishes.

In her place is a sheep.

I gasp. Clover didn't chew the moly. She wasn't pro-tected. And the mist turns people into sheep. Shoe runs to her, wrapping her arms around Clover's now-wooly neck.

I spin to the woman standing in the doorway. She's

tiny, with a beautiful, distant face and long pale hair hanging straight, blinking up at us calmly. "Change her back!" I yell, right in her face. "Change her back right now!"

She sighs. "No," she says firmly, and closes the door.

I look at Clover-who-is-a-sheep, terror rolling through me. "No," I repeat. "No no no." The sheep stares back, with a black, furry face and sad eyes. Shoe whispers in her ear, but it doesn't do anything.

"I'll get her to change Clover back," Peter says. "Don't worry." But his voice wavers.

I knock on the door again, frantically. After a minute of solid knocking, it opens.

"What do you want, and why haven't you changed to sheep?" she snaps. "I don't like visitors."

I take a deep breath. I need to be calm. I need to get the words right. I need to save Clover. I clench my fists, so tight I can feel my nails digging into my skin.

"Scylla sent me," I say. My voice is wavery too. "She's down below, in the water, and would like to speak with you." I breathe, clench my fists. Breathe, clench. I feel the pressure building in my chest. "But first you need to change my sister back."

She opens the door wider and tilts her head. "Scylla. *That* is interesting." Her voice is low and smooth, buttery. She has a little bit of an accent, but I'd never be able to place it. "It has been a long age since I had an appeal about Scylla. But you are a mortal. Are you not afraid of the monster?"

I swallow hard. "No, ma'am."

She raises an eyebrow, and I wonder if I said the wrong thing. If she's going to produce a monster I *will* be afraid of.

"You did not change, so you are protected. Herbs, no doubt." She opens the door all the way. "Come in, and we will discuss it."

Peter puts a hand on the door.

"Wait." I stop him and shake my head. It feels like a trap. "We would rather stay out here, ma'am. Please change my sister back now, and then I will take you to where Scylla is."

She laughs. "You're a wily one. Won't cross the threshold, eh? Very well." She glances at Peter. "You should have known better also. I see you know the ways of things." She smiles at him. "But you are eager and confident. You remind me of Odysseus."

She turns back to me. "I suppose Scylla desires me to change her to her former shape as well?"

I nod. Clover bleats, which makes me shudder.

"Listen how prettily she sings for *me* now," Circe says.

I bite my lip. She knows Clover sings, somehow . . . that she sang for Scylla. I wonder if she knows everything.

She tilts her head again. "My flock is getting low," she says. "You must answer a riddle correctly, or you will all stay and be my sheep."

I swallow. Shoe gulps, her eyes wide. Peter nods once.

"A riddle," I say quietly. "Okay."

Because there's always a riddle, in a story. I just hope I've read enough stories to know the answer.

Still Fergus

(because Clover is a sheep)

Circe steps neatly out the door and sits on a bumpy mound of grass in front of her house. She opens one hand, and Clover trots over to her, like a dog, and lies down, her sheep legs curled under her. Circe idly strokes Clover's wool. It makes me feel ill.

Peter steps forward, fists raised. "Stop that," he growls. "She's not a pet."

Shoe steps up next to him. "Let her go."

Circe blinks at us, eyes round and innocent, but then she shrugs, and Clover bounds up again, retreating to the edge of the mist. She bleats sadly. "When you fail to guess the riddle, you will all be my pets," Circe says. She smiles, scary, like a shark's smile.

I have a sudden image of her color, which isn't really a color at all: bright, blinding white. With a little gold mixed in.

"What's the riddle?" I ask.

She studies us again, then points at Peter and Shoe. "You two step away. The riddle is for the mortal boy, so he can save his sister. Not for you."

Shoe scowls, and Peter turns bright red again.

"Okay," I say. "Okay."

Uh-oh. I feel like I'm losing my words, like my brain is starting to spin. But it can't right now. I have to think, to be able to solve this riddle. I have to listen, and understand.

Peter and Shoe reluctantly move back a few steps.

Circe smiles again, all shark. "Are you ready? You will only get one answer."

I nod. I probably look calm, though inside I'm screaming.

She folds her hands. "The riddle: *The beginning of eternity, the end of time and space. The beginning of every end, and the end of every place.*" She laughs. "One Fergus, one Clover. There, you have an extra hint from me, as a bonus."

My mind blurs, and I want to run and hide somewhere quiet.

No. Not now. Focus.

I tap my fingers, trying to focus, to think. I've heard this before somewhere, or something like it. But I can't quite connect anything. I look back at Peter and Shoe. Shoe gives me a half smile, encouraging.

Peter tugs on his ears. I hope that's not a clue, because I don't understand it.

Think.

The beginning of eternity, the end of time and space. Not the obvious, the big bang or anything like that. That's not how riddles work. It's a trick. Something small, hidden in the clue. The beginning of every end. Every end. End. Endings? The endings of places? Of stories?

The endings of words?

The beginning of every end. The end of every place. One Fergus, one Clover. I take a deep breath and let it out slowly: one . . . two . . . three. She should have said one *in* Fergus, one *in* Clover. One in one.

I glance down. Circe is watching me, smoothing her hair with one pale hand.

I smile, and the stress leaks away. I got it.

"You see two in every week," I answer, "and one in every year, but never in a day."

Circe sighs. Her face is still, like a mask. "Say it aloud."

"The letter *E*," I say, triumphant.

Circe pushes herself up. "Yes."

Shoe and Peter cheer. I feel the happiness bubble up. I saved her! I solved it.

"I will only transform one," Circe says slyly. "Clover or Scylla. Which will you choose?"

The bubble bursts. This is another trick, of course. A god's trick. Scylla has been a monster for hundreds of years. Thousands of years. Clover has only been a sheep for a couple of minutes. If I choose Clover, Circe will not have lost anything. If I choose Scylla . . .

Obviously I can't choose Scylla.

"My sister," I say quietly.

"Very well." She blinks, and Clover stands there again, unharmed, staring at her hands. Shoe rips the bag off her waist and throws it to Clover, and Clover swallows a handful of each herb fast, to protect herself from the mist.

Circe looks at each of us in turn. "Done. I believe that is the end of our dealings." She steps inside and closes the green door again, with a click.

Shoe runs to Clover and hugs her, hard. Clover hugs back for a long moment, but then she lets go.

"That was my fault," she says quietly. "You traded Scylla's chance for me because I was too scared to come up with you, and then I was careless because I wanted to be part of the adventure. We have to try again. Scylla still has Jasmina and Allora trapped in her cave. She won't release them unless we succeed." Tears fill her eyes. "We have to try again."

I shake my head. "Once the gods make a deal, it's done."

"She is right, though," Peter says. "We must finish the adventure. We cannot abandon the mermaids now."

Clover turns to me. "Circe made a deal with you. Your deal is complete. She didn't make a deal with me." She strides up and knocks on the door, even harder than I did.

"No," Circe calls from inside. "We are done. Leave me alone, boy."

"It's not the boy," Clover says loudly. "It's the girl you turned into a sheep. And I want to make a bargain with you for Scylla."

"You can't make a bargain," I say to Clover, the words spilling out. "It'll go wrong. Don't."

She presses her lips together in a thin line and knocks once more. "You'll want to hear it," she calls.

The door opens, and Circe leans against the door-frame, her arms folded. "Yes?"

"No," I hiss.

Clover glances at me. "I'll offer you something in exchange," she says carefully. "If you change Scylla to her former self. I'll offer you something that means everything to me."

Circe raises her eyebrows. "Yes?" she repeats.

Clover clenches her fists, and takes a deep breath, then another. "I'll give you my voice," she says. "My singing."

Clover

Circe tilts her head, like she's considering. "You offer your singing?"

"I *can* sing," I say. "It's the one thing I can do."

"Stop!" Fergus shouts.

"*Can* you?" Circe asks. She laughs, a mean, small laugh. "That would be more helpful with Scylla and her dogs, I would think. Or Ursula. I imagine that's where you got the idea." She shakes her head. "I have no need for a singer or a voice. What would I do with your voice?"

"What do you want, then?" I ask desperately.

Circe doesn't answer.

Shoe looks at me for a moment, then steps forward. "I could stay with you here. I can fix things. Or I could . . . take care of the animals."

"No!" I whisper.

"No one would miss me," she says, soft. "Not really. And if it would help you and free the mermaids . . ." Her eyes are bright. "It would be an adventure."

I reach out and take her hand, and she squeezes it. She's a wonderful friend. But I can't let her do that alone. It was my fault, not hers.

I swallow hard. Don't think. Don't worry. Just do. "I . . . I could stay too. We could be your companions. Helpers."

"No!" Fergus yells. "No no no!"

I look at him. "I'm sorry," I say. But it's clear that he doesn't need me anymore, not in Neverland. He would be all right.

I can't think about Mom. About home, about everything I'd be letting go. I just can't let Jasmina, Allora, Shoe—and even Scylla—lose their whole lives because of me.

Circe's face changes, intent on mine. "You would sacrifice yourself for the monster, truly?" She nods at Shoe. "You would sacrifice yourself? This is not a trick or a joke. Pan will not come rescue you in a week's time."

Peter grimaces, like he was thinking that.

"It's not a trick," I say.

"We promise," Shoe echoes.

Peter steps forward, next to me. "You have no need of them, Circe," he says. "You know it. I will give you something of Neverland instead, something of power." He draws the sword from his back and lays it flat across his hands. "It is the magical sword Skofnung. It is harder than any other sword, does not rust, and is always sharp." He winks at Fergus. "I stole it from the Danes. It has been in Neverland for nearly ever. Take it instead, as payment for Scylla."

"But why?" Circe asks. "Why would any of you offer these things? You could ask to go back to Neverland—or home—right now, and never see Scylla again. Why offer your life, or even your sword, for a monster?"

Everyone turns to me, and I take a sharp breath. Again it feels like being called on, like a test. It's important how I answer. I think hard about what to say.

Scylla is a monster on the outside. She dragged me under the water. She blinded me. She used to kill people.

But I feel for her. She didn't choose to look the way she does. She was cursed. After everyone rejected her because they were afraid of her, she still tried to stop hurting others. She hid herself away in a cave with her art. Even when she stole us, she was only trying to get rest.

"She's holding the mermaids," I say slowly. "But also, she needs help. I don't think anyone's ever tried to help her." I look at Shoe and Peter and Fergus. We've helped each other every step of the way. Scylla deserves that too.

Circe looks at us for a long time, all four of us, then lifts her chin and stares off into the distance, at the sea. None of us speak, or move. Shoe holds my hand tightly. At last Circe sighs, raises one finger, and disappears into her house, letting the door swing slowly shut behind her. The sheep bleat in the distance, and the mist swirls around our feet.

"You can't stay here," Fergus whispers. "You can't."

"I don't want to," I say. Tears burn my eyes. "But we have to save Allora and Jasmina. And Scylla . . ." I sigh. "Like I said, she needs someone to help her. I can't steal her one chance."

Circe is gone for a long time, long enough that I start to worry she won't come out again. Then the door opens and she's there, a green glass bottle in her hand.

"This is what I want," she says quietly. We all wait, breathless. "This kind of loyalty. That is what I have always wanted." She starts walking toward the cliff ladder, fast. We follow her, tumbling after her as well as we can.

"You know the story of Odysseus?" Circe asks. "He was happy on my island. I was happy, feasting all his men. But they abandoned me and left me alone. And all the others: they came, they visited, and then they left, moving on with their lives. No one stayed. No one was loyal to me." She stops and smooths the hair on her shoulder, studying Fergus and Peter, then Shoe, then me.

"You"—she points at Fergus—"you would sacrifice yourself for your sister. And you"—she points at me, and my heart skips—"you would sacrifice your voice, then yourself, for what everyone else sees as only a monster."

Circe looks at me a moment longer. Then she points at Shoe. "You offered to give up your life for your friends. And you . . ." She points at Peter. Then she laughs. "You are Pan. You have no loyalty to anything but Neverland, in truth. Yet you offered the sword of Skofnung. It is no small gift, for Pan."

Peter grins, like they're sharing a secret.

Circe starts walking again. "Now it is time for all of you to leave. I am tired of visitors."

My stomach tightens. She's rejecting our offers. We failed, and it's my fault.

"Please," I start, but Circe waves a hand, cutting me off. We get to the cliff, the place where the rope ladder is slung under a boulder. She steps right up to the edge, her toes curling over.

"Scylla!" Her voice booms, cracking across the waves like thunder. Fergus covers his ears. I want to. "Scylla! Show yourself."

Far down below, by the shore, Scylla pops to the surface like a cork, dogs barking madly. She raises both hands, palms high, like she's praying to Circe. "Please, great goddess—" she says.

"Stop," Circe interrupts, still in that thundering voice. "These children have done the arguing for you. Stay where you are." She pulls the stopper out of the green bottle, raises it up, says something I don't understand, then tosses it down, the bottle curving into the water next to Scylla. It lands with a tiny splash. Scylla looks at it, gasps, and dives underwater.

"Did you—" Fergus starts, but Circe interrupts again.

"Watch," she says.

We watch, silent. The water thrashes and churns. Fergus reaches out and touches my hand. I touch back, lightly, then let go. After a very long time—my feet go numb—Scylla's head pops up again.

It's a normal head. No eels. No dogs barking either, just perfect silence. Scylla looks down at herself, rubs her hands along her waist, and squeals in glee. She raises both arms again to the cliff. "Thank you!" she calls. "Oh, thank you. Thank you too, Fergus. Clover. Neverland folk."

Circe waves a hand, and Scylla is gone. Disappeared. I spin to Circe. "Where did she go?"

She sighs and slides the stopper into a pocket. "I sent her home to her father. They have much to catch up on." She smiles. When she means it, she has a smile that makes me want to grin back and dance. Like Peter's, but stronger. "Your mermaids are home too, sight restored. It was easily done."

"Thank you!" I say. Fergus, Shoe, and even Peter echo me.

Circe tilts her head. "You were loyal, when you did not have to be. And you saw through to her inside, to the person she was before I meddled. I decided it was time to let her be that again." She sighs and brushes her hands together. "Now I would like to be alone. It is surely time you returned to your home also, is it not? Your mother is worried."

"How do you know about our mother?" Fergus asks.

Circe laughs. "I am a goddess, and a witch besides." She touches me under the chin, then Fergus. "I will send you, brave ones. To Neverland, or England?"

"Neverland," Fergus says before I can answer.

The sadness grips me again. He really is going to stay in Neverland, isn't he? He's going to send me home alone.

A moment later we're surrounded by blinding white light. When I open my eyes, the four of us are on the beach at Neverland, the lagoon sparkling in the sunlight.

Fergus

The breeze from the lagoon is warm and wet against my cheeks. I laugh. I lean my head back and howl, and Peter and Shoe join in, the three of us in chorus like real wolves. It feels amazing, letting everything out. I howl again, long and loud. We did it!

Clover goes down to the shore. A few of the mermaids pop up, crying out in what sounds like happiness—then all of them come, including Jasmina and Allora. Clover talks to them, her arms waving, telling them of the adventure. Shoe goes too, running down with her arms wide. I stay high up on the beach with Peter, so I won't want to go in the water. I've had enough of water for a while.

"Lost Boys!" Peter calls. "Come!"

In the next minute the pixies find us, a whole swarm of them, flitting around Peter and me. I let my hands fly, zipping in and out around the pixies, like a dance.

I'm so glad we saved Scylla. But I'm more glad Clover and I came out okay, as people and not sheep. Now I just want to celebrate with Peter, and Friendly, and Shoe, and the rest of them.

When I hear the footsteps thundering over the hill and see Friendly with his sun smile, and Jumper and Swim and Rella and George, joy surges inside me. I hold on to it, grasping the joy tight.

The Lost Boys surround me, whooping and shouting. George starts a dance, and Rella and Swim join in. I dance too, waving my hands, jerking my feet, moving however I want. It's free, open. It's so easy to just *be*, here.

I'm not sure I want to go back to the real world, where people stare if I even tap my fingers.

Shoe and Clover are still down on the shore, talking with their heads close together, and then hugging. Then they run back too, and everybody congratulates Clover and Shoe. All of us dance for a while, arms raised, spinning. Two of the pixies circle around me, their warmth like more friends.

"The travelers are back from our adventure, victorious!" Peter shouts. "Huzzah!"

"Huzzah!" we all echo. The word feels buzzy on my tongue, and I say it again, quieter. "Huzzah! Huzzah!"

"Now," Peter says, and we all stop, and quiet down. "We must tell you the story."

Everyone drops down into a circle on the sand. Peter looks at me and nods.

Me?

Yes, I will tell it.

The words come. I tell from when Scylla took us underwater, with Clover filling in the details for her part. When we tell about Clover being turned into a sheep, they all ooh. Shoe puts an arm around Clover's shoulders, and Clover leans into her.

When I'm done, there's a silence. A good silence, like the hushed moment after a play. Then they all cheer.

"It was a good adventure," Peter says. He seems like his normal self again, now that he's back in Neverland. Cheerful, relaxed, and confident. "We must Feast tonight! And tomorrow, perhaps we will ride the stream. Even though it is dragon season. You have faced a sea monster and a witch; surely you can face a dragon!"

They all cheer again, and I cheer too.

Except Clover, who raises her hand. "Isn't it . . . ,"

she says softly. She looks around at all of us, at me. "Isn't it time for us to go home?"

This kind of silence is not good. It's uncomfortable. Friendly looks out at the ocean, and Jumper and George start playing with the sand. Peter clears his throat.

"We thought perhaps you might like to stay," he says. He lifts his chin. "At least Fergus. If you want to go home, Clover, I will take you."

Clover's eyes fill with tears. I look down at the sand, at the circle of bare, dirty, happy feet. I don't want to see her cry. I don't want to *make* her cry.

"Fergus?" she says, her voice quivering. "Do you want to stay here?"

I stare harder at the sand, at the flecks of quartz that sparkle, and turn the question over in my mind.

Part of me does want to stay. I love being here. I can do whatever I want, be who I am, and no one questions it. They accept it, celebrate my flying hands and my spins and even my pauses. The pixie helped me through a meltdown, and I know it would again, if I wanted it. I think all of them would help.

Clover and Mom accept me too, but in a different way. They still worry a little what other people think. They still assume I can't do as much as I can, and Clover hovers over me too much. Way too much. And other people . . . There are good ones, like my friends at the Autism Center, and Grandmother. But lots of people just stare. Laugh. Don't even try to understand or be patient. The real world is harsh sometimes.

I could stay here and be free from all that, forever. Just dance and sing and shout and adventure and feast and *be*.

But I would never see Mom again—or Clover. I wouldn't go back to school. I'd never learn anything else about the gods and goddesses, find any more books at the library, or see the British Museum. I want to go to college someday. I want to teach, maybe, about the myths. Or work with the artifacts, at a museum. Eventually I want to grow up and be a man. A husband. A dad.

If I stayed here, it would be like hiding instead of facing the world.

"I think we should Feast," I say, and look up. Clover has tears dripping down her cheeks. "And then we should both go home, together."

38

Clover

We fly all night, Peter and Fergus and the pixies and me . . . and Shoe. When we were on the beach at Neverland, she said she realized after meeting us that she was ready to grow up. If we could do it, she could too. She wanted to see London for real. She wanted to have a real family . . . maybe even a mother. She wanted to learn more than she could in Neverland.

She even picked out a new name for herself while we were flying. She decided she would be Wendy.

I don't know what will happen to her in our world, but I know Grandmother will be pleased.

We fly and fly. When we finally get to Grandmother

and Grandfather's house, the sky is still mostly dark, the sun just starting to rise. The window of the nursery is open, waiting. We fly in, one at a time, and land lightly on the wooden floor. Fergus and I drop our backpacks. We didn't really need them after all.

Mom is lying across one of the beds, asleep, the blowing curtains almost touching her face.

I squeak, and she sits up, blinking. "Mom!" I yell, and launch myself at her. She opens her arms wide and I lose myself in a hug for a little while. I feel Fergus next to me too, leaning against Mom. Her tears drip on my head.

"You're okay," she says. "Both of you. You're okay."

"I always bring them back safe," Peter says, a bit sharply. I sit up, though I stay with Mom's arm around my waist, and Fergus stands only a step away. I'd almost forgotten for a second that Peter was still here. That Shoe was here. "Hello, Wendy," he says.

Mom tucks her hair behind her ears. "Gwen," she corrects. "Hello, Peter."

"You *can* see me," he says. "You always pretended not to when I came."

She looks down, smoothing the blanket that's already smooth. "I am very angry with you for taking them, Peter. When you knew I wouldn't approve."

"Are you?" Great-Aunt Tilly stands in the doorway.

252

"Or are you glad they had their adventure? You should be. Look at them. They're happy."

"Great-Aunt Tilly!" I smile at her from Mom's arms.

"Tilly!" Peter shouts. "Good to see you again."

Great-Aunt Tilly grins at him, and for a moment she looks young. "You look exactly the same."

Peter tilts his head in acknowledgment, and I suddenly get it. Tilly must have been a Lost Boy too. Like Shoe. She decided to come here and grow up, with Grandmother.

"Gwen, Tilly," Peter says, "this is Wendy. She has chosen to live here now." He touches Shoe—Wendy—on the shoulder. "You will be happy as a grown-up?"

She smiles, her eyes shining. "I will be happy. Thank you, Peter. Thank you for everything."

He nods. "And you will take care of her?" he asks Mom.

"I will," Grandmother says from the doorway. She and Tilly stand close to each other, arms linked together. She beams at Wendy, at all of us. "I'd love to."

"And me," Tilly says. "We shall raise her the rest of the way together."

Peter smiles at them both with his small-toothed grin. "Hello, Margaret. I'd bring you both back with me again in a flash if I could."

Grandmother sighs. I think she'd go back, too.

Peter reaches out his hands, palms up, and Fergus and I go over and each take one.

"I will return," he says. He looks at each of us, solemn. "So you must visit this place from time to time. I will watch for you. And we can go to Neverland and have more adventures. Yes?" The pixies zip around us.

"Yes!" Fergus smiles so wide it fills his face. "Yes yes yes!"

"Yes," I say. I'd like to see Jasmina and Allora and the other mermaids again. And maybe ride the stream when it's not dragon season.

I look at Mom, and she looks at Great-Aunt Tilly and Grandmother. She nods once.

No one tells Mom that Peter wanted us to stay. That Fergus almost stayed. But we came back, so maybe it doesn't matter.

"I'm sorry we interrupted your studying," I whisper to Mom.

She smiles, shaky. "It's okay now. I'll pass. You can help me finish studying here."

Peter lets go of our hands. He hops to the windowsill and stands framed in it for a moment, facing us all. "Till next time, then. To Neverland!" he says, and he and the pixies launch into the air, and away.

Fergus, Wendy, and I run to the window and watch

him go, a small shape flying out over the city, as the sun peeks above the horizon. Mom stands behind us, her hand warm on my shoulder. I'm glad to be home, safe with my family.

But I'm awfully glad we went.

"To Neverland," Fergus says.

"To Neverland," I whisper. "And back home again."

Acknowledgments

This book and these characters mean so very much to me.

Fergus and Clover came to me whole in an entirely different setting, and I knew I needed to tell their story. When I realized they were descendants of Wendy, it all clicked into place and became this joyful book about a boy who is autistic and his anxious, bossy sister—but also about Peter Pan and mythology and sea monsters and mermaids and pixies and goddesses and Lost Boys, some of whom are girls. (Shoe is one of my new favorite people.) I hope you love them all as much as I do.

Thank you to my editor, Jenna Lettice, for her unwavering enthusiasm and support, thoughtful notes, and inspiring emails with Peter Pan GIFs. Thank you to Michelle Nagler for just the right suggestion. Huge thanks to the Random House team, including George

Ermos, who created the amazing cover; designer Bob Bianchini; interior designer Trish Parcell; copyeditors Barbara Bakowski and Alison Kolani; and publicist Emily Bamford (who did such a tremendous job with *Nutcracked*!). Thank you to Lyn Miller-Lachmann for valuable feedback.

Thank you to Kate Schafer Testerman, who always has my back, no matter what. Also for hugs over the phone and in person when they're most needed.

All my love to Michael and Sophie, who make it possible and make it worthwhile.

I did my very best to make sure that both Fergus and Clover were real, true kids, not stereotypes of any kind. I read books, blogs, websites, and posts and watched videos posted by autistic people themselves. I wanted their inside perspective, not an outside view from parents, therapists, or "experts" on what autistic kids are like. I listened to members of the ActuallyAutistic community on how they want to be represented, and that awareness was always in my mind. I'd like to recommend the Useful Resources section for further information, real talk, and wonderful stories. Please read more, and read widely! Any errors are my own.

To the readers of this book: you really are perfect as you are.

Useful Resources

Nonfiction

Bascom, Julia, and others. *Loud Hands: Autistic People, Speaking.* Washington, DC: The Autistic Press, 2012.

Grandin, Temple. *Thinking in Pictures.* New York: Doubleday, 1995.

Higashida, Naoki. *The Reason I Jump: The Inner Voice of a Thirteen-Year-Old Boy with Autism.* New York: Random House, 2013.

Robinson, John Elder. *Look Me in the Eye: My Life with Asperger's.* New York: Crown, 2007.

Silberman, Steve. *Neurotribes: The Legacy of Autism and the Future of Neurodiversity.* New York: Avery, 2015.

Fiction

Baskin, Nora Raleigh. *Anything but Typical.* New York: Simon and Schuster Books for Young Readers, 2009.

Lucas, Rachael. *The State of Grace.* New York: Feiwel and Friends, 2018.

Pla, Sally J. *The Someday Birds.* New York: Harper, 2017.

Ursu, Anne. *The Real Boy.* New York: Walden Pond Press, 2013.

Websites and Social Media

#ActuallyAutistic community

Aspergers Girl: youtube.com/user/EvieMayB/videos

Autism Mythbusters: autismmythbusters.com

Autistic Self Advocacy Network: autisticadvocacy.org

Ballastexistenz: ballastexistenz.wordpress.com

Dear Neurotypicals: dearneurotypicals.tumblr.com

Disability in Kidlit (articles and reviews): disabilityinkidlit.com

Just a Skinny Boy, Autism and Me playlist (videos may contain adult language): youtube.com/user /justaskinnyboy/playlists

Just Stimming: juststimming.wordpress.com

Little Hux Tales: huxtales.wordpress.com/category/autism, @littlehux)

Musings of an Aspie: musingsofanaspie.com

Neurowonderful: neurowonderful.tumblr.com (blog) and youtube.com/user/neurowonderful/featured (Ask an Autistic)

Non-Speaking Autistic Speaking: nonspeakingautisticspeaking.blogspot.com

The Stimming Checklist, "So what IS stimming?": what-is-stimming.org/so-what-is-stimming

Thinking Person's Guide to Autism: www.thinkingautismguide.com

About the Author

Susan Adrian is a fourth-generation Californian who now lives in the beautiful Big Sky country of Montana. During college she spent a year abroad at the University of Sussex in England—which started a lifelong fascination with all things British, particularly British stories for kids. These days she splits her time as a writer, scientific editor, and mom. Susan is the author of the holiday fantasy *Nutcracked* and two thrilling books for teens. She also keeps busy researching fun stuff, traveling, and writing more books. She's been to London many times but hasn't yet been invited to Neverland.

susanadrian.net
@susan_adrian